The
Secret of Saramount

The
Secret of Saramount

LILLIAN CHEATHAM

DOUBLEDAY & COMPANY, INC.

GARDEN CITY, NEW YORK

1978

All of the characters in the book
are fictitious, and any resemblance
to actual persons, living or dead,
is purely coincidental.

Library of Congress Cataloging in Publication Data

Cheatham, Lillian.
The secret of Saramount.

I. Title.
PZ4.C5138Se   [PS3553.H384]   813′.5′4
ISBN 0-385-12720-0
Library of Congress Catalog Card Number 76–56275

FOR
Laurence Hutton

The

Secret of Saramount

CHAPTER 1

I would like to go to Saramount again someday to see if the ghosts have been laid, but I do not know if I have the courage. My one visit back was not a success. The mellowed walls held too many memories: I reached out and touched the dead as I passed through the spacious old rooms; I heard their voices even as I fled the house to stand upon the banks of the river and gaze across the abandoned ricefields that stretch toward the distant beaches and the sea. In the end, I could not bear it; I found myself weeping like a child and begging to be taken home.

Unlike Saramount, however, my memories of Colin are, happily, good ones, and they come at odd moments, as when I am in the midst of my rocketing merry family. The baby will put her hand confidingly in mine; for a fleeting instant I see myself in her face, and I am back at Saramount with Colin, in the hot southern summertime. As the voices fade, Colin and I are children again at Saramount.

It is then that I must take myself sternly in hand with the reminder that I am no longer that child, and I have my own young family growing up around me now. Occasionally, in their quieter moments, which occur all too infrequently nowadays, they cluster around my knee and beg for stories of Saramount, of Colin and Grandfather and Mammy, and the deep black river with its swamp and alligators, all so different from the cool, green forests they know. Then my stories grow more vivid with each telling until even I have difficulty in knowing the truth, but I am careful of their tender years: Saramount has no shadows for the children.

But sometimes, particularly in the spring, my mind drifts back to other days, other times. A single small thing can trigger my thoughts: it may be nothing more than the rich earthy odor of a new-plowed field or the sound of church bells, sweet and clear, on a still Sunday morning, borne across the valley from distant hills. And then, caught, suspended on a moment of time as swift and transient as the upbeat of a bird's wing, I remember . . .

I remember the train ride from the school that had been my home for most of my eighteen years, and I have a sigh and a twinge of sympathy for the person I was then. At all times impetuous, I was on that day seething with excitement, yet nevertheless forced to remain modestly seated with my actions under stern control, as befitting my new adult status. Silent and decorous though I might be, I could and I would think of Colin, his name repeating itself in my brain to the sound of clacking wheels and throbbing engine, and I have a vivid recollection of leaning forward and smiling at my reflection again and again in the black rushing window.

I was on my way to Saramount and nothing could stop me now. The last goodbye had been said and I had been placed on the train in care of the conductor and his red-capped porter. Not the most desirable mode of travel for a well-brought-up young lady of the day, but under the circumstances, the best when no suitable escort could be located at the last minute. I had been carefully settled in my stateroom: my meals ordered and proper reading material of an uplifting nature placed at hand, all by Miss Warren herself. The parting had been reluctant, for it was not the way the headmistress cared to see a Millhaven girl return home, but then, unusual circumstances called for unusual measures, and one must make do with what lay at hand. Her pupil was being met by family, and urgency was the order of the day.

In my ten years' tenancy at Millhaven, a girls' boarding school located in the mountains of western Virginia, I had never before traveled alone. Grandfather or my cousin Victor had always accompanied me to a centrally located city, usually Raleigh, and there a group of my fellow classmates and I would meet a teacher from the school, to be chaperoned for the remainder of the trip. It might be 1910, with women marching in parades and rallying the vote, but I was still hedged in by the restrictions of Grandfather's bygone era. Now, with Miss Warren's exhortations still in my ears, I was too timid to think of venturing out into the train's dining room or even the corridor. As my bedtime approached, I was finding it hard to settle down, for I had been living on the thin edge of hysteria since that morning, and the long-distance telephone call which had precipitated me into this unexpected journey.

The news of the call itself had been enough to resound through the school with all the speed and impact of a cannon shot. Although parents were informed at the outset that a telephone was available in the Head's office for the use of the pupils, the fact was that Miss Warren encouraged no one to use it, least of all herself. Certainly, it was totally unexpected that the first such call should be received by Sarah Mountain, one of the senior pupils, and one in whom, heretofore, there had been such a sad lack of interest: one who had remained at the school, year after year, when other students went home for the Christmas holidays, and whom, although her gifts from home had been lavish, and her pin money and clothing allowance generous, it was sadly apparent that her presence there was not wanted.

So it was that, when I obeyed the summons to Miss Warren's office and saw how nervously she was eying the receiver dangling from the wall behind her desk, I was too overcome to speak. And when, finally, I did, I found myself screaming at my unseen partner.

It was Madeline. When I heard her voice, I assumed there had been an accident to Grandfather and we lost a precious minute while she assured me there had not been, and that she was calling me at his bidding.

"He wants you to come home immediately, Sarah. He has notified Uncle Charles and Rose, and he wants all of the family at Saramount as soon as possible."

I couldn't take it in. "Before I graduate?" I asked stupidly.

"Yes. At once. You must be on the earliest train. You see, it is Colin. He has come home." Her voice faded, or perhaps it was the sudden faintness that threatened to overcome me. By a supreme effort of will, I remained standing, consciously willing her voice back. And when it returned, it was strongly, on the end of a phrase: ". . . just as though he had never been away."

"Sister"—I was desperately calm, calling her by Grandfather's pet name. "What did you say to me?"

"Sarah, you aren't listening! I am already speaking as loudly as I can. I said that Colin had returned, and Grandfather wants you to come home. He wants everyone home. That means Uncle Charles and Rose too. She had already sailed from France, so he cabled her ship, telling her to come on directly to Charleston. But I told you all of that." I recognized the querulous note in Madeline's voice, as though she questioned the wisdom of telling me anything. "Now, get your wits together, Sarah. You have too much to do to waste your time dreaming. You must prepare to leave school right away. Your train will be met."

I listened in a daze, guilty of the dreaming of which I had been accused, while she continued with further instructions. Then, recognizing that she was preparing to close the conversation, I sought desperately to prolong it. "Sister, Sister, please don't hang up. You must tell me about Colin. What happened? When—" I wanted to shriek, but I schooled myself to speak calmly.

But Madeline's voice, cool and remote, had already faded again and I only heard a word or two, then " . . . later," and distinctly, "but Victor says he is an impostor."

That was all. And how like Madeline to leave me with those words! I screamed at her to come back, but only the humming sound of the miles between us answered me. Miss Warren had to take the receiver gently from me and break the connection.

But the call had been, by its nature, important enough, the summons urgent enough to put me on the late-afternoon train, bound for Talley and home. I had wanted to leave at once, willy-nilly, without any luggage, but the earlier train would have arrived at midnight, and although I pleaded with Miss Warren to be allowed to take it, she was adamant in refusing. Talley was not Saramount: I would have a distance of three miles to walk, for she was sure my grandfather would not expect me at such an hour.

However, a woman such as Miss Warren can, when the occasion demands it, move mountains, and she easily had me ready by the time of the next train, in spite of my secret, mounting certainty that somehow, at the last moment, I would be delayed. A certain formality was demanded of my leavetaking: my trunk must be packed properly, corded and taken away to await me at the station: I took my last meal with the other pupils in the dining room: a box lunch was prepared to delay the inevitable meal that I must eat with the unknown, and possibly libertine, passengers on the train; and then, lastly, coated and hatted and wearing my best navy skirt and white waist, I was placed aboard by Miss Warren herself.

She warned me of all the possible methods of assault that might be made upon my virtue; she even placed an umbrella nearby, in lieu of a hatpin, for protection; she showed me the facilities of my drawing room, and then, with just enough time to say goodbye, she hesitantly introduced the subject foremost in both our minds.

"The young man who has returned is Colin, your cousin, who has been missing for so long?" she asked, although I was sure she already knew the answer.

"Yes, ma'am."

"I have long deplored your impetuosity, Sarah Elizabeth," she said chidingly. "It is one of your more undesirable traits I have tried to eradicate, and in this case it could cause you a lot of grief. I have always been aware of your —er—preoccupation with your cousin's disappearance"— her voice delicately stressed her distaste and invoked overtones of impropriety. "You should remember, however, that he has not remained the same person he was when he went away. After all, it has been—how long?—twelve years. He will have changed by now, of course. I hope you will think of that, and prepare yourself not to be disappointed."

She must have seen from my blank face how little impression she was making, for she sighed and her expression softened. For the first time in ten years she allowed herself to press a cool cheek to mine and pat my shoulder. "Never mind that, child. I hope everything will go well for you. Remember, I shall always be happy to see you if you have occasion to come back."

And then she was gone, hurried to the platform by an anxious porter. And if she thought I'd forget her the instant she left, she was mistaken, for I wasted all of a minute thinking of her with rueful fondness. For ten years she had guided me in the principles and foundations laid down in her excellent school, and she had taught me her own sound precepts of moral and social behavior and intellectual attainment. I knew that I had cause to be grateful to her. But not tonight. Tonight I merely wanted to think of Colin.

The sky, which had been lowering all day, had turned slate-gray and it began to rain, trickling greasy rivulets in twisted patterns across the smoke-blackened windowpane. Twilight would be early today, and indeed it was not long before the porter knocked and came in to light the swaying coal-oil lamp over my head.

"Mighty nice meal in th' dinah tonight, miss," he coaxed invitingly. "Mighty nice terr'pin soup. Mighty good rabbit pie tonight, miss."

But I had been provided with a box lunch and, besides, had been warned by Miss Warren that I must, at all costs, avoid the diner in the evening, where wine was served and the animal, which raged at all times in man's breast, might propel him into an act of passion upon seeing a young, unchaperoned girl. So I nibbled cold fried chicken and biscuits, and looked out my window at the darkening sky and the receding mountains. I could not have eaten dinner, anyway. I was too excited for food when I thought of what lay ahead of me on the morrow.

With the coming of complete darkness, I rang for the porter to make up my bed. He came quickly and, while he worked, gave me some paternal advice.

"Not a thing in this worl' to worry 'bout, miss. Th' conductor an' me, we jes within hailin' beck 'n' call. One of us neahby all night. Jes you lock this doah aftah me an' ain't nobody kin git in heah tonight!"

When he left, I realized how tired I was. I brushed out my

hair, braided it, and put on my flannel dressing gown over my petticoat. Within two minutes of lying down, I was asleep.

I was still tired when the porter's knock awakened me, but his words brought me upright.

"Talley, miss. Bettah hurry!"

Until I stepped off the train and stood alone on the dark, empty platform, I had assumed that Victor or Grandfather would be there to meet me with the buggy. The porter dithered after lowering my trunk, hesitating to leave me unattended, but the train gave a warning whistle and with an apologetic, "Sorry, miss," he swung back on.

Which was another strange thing. Even the whistle, clear and piercing in the still night, had no effect on the closed, darkened windows of Talley. It was no more than a hamlet of perhaps fifty souls, but all trains were accompanied by a bustle of activity and intense interest from the town's inhabitants. Although the midnight train stopped only through prior arrangement, there had never been a time, within my knowledge, when the stationmaster was not there, and some of the town lights did not spring up.

But it was an oddity which I barely noted. The dark station did not frighten me, nor did the walk ahead. I had walked that distance from Talley to Saramount many times and I could do it again. Leaving my trunk where it stood and pinning up the hem of my skirt so that it would not trail in the dust, I stepped out confidently, thankful that I had not yielded to the temptation to wear my new kid boots with the two-inch heels.

There was a harvest moon, hanging low and full in the rim of the sky, and I was glad of its light, for it bleached the road white as it ran, straight as a ribbon, through the trees. At times, those trees met overhead, blocking out the moonlight, and it was only my memory of each turn and twist that guided my footsteps. I could have paced each foot of it blindfolded, for as I walked, Colin walked with me, my companion in the strange, dreamy stillness.

And it was so still, with the darkness like a muffling blanket, smothering all the familiar small noises that one hears on a spring night in the country. I listened for an owl's hoot, or the rustle of a bird's wing, or the sound of singing insects, but I listened in vain. The moss hung in motionless black strings from the trees. I passed the churchyard, with its forlorn little church and the gray tombstones occupying their centuries-old position in the long, tangled grass, and I looked for Joe Bob Harrison, who, on nights like this one, when the moon was bright, finished a bottle while lying between his parents' graves, but the churchyard was empty and the dead slept on, heedless and uncaring.

The road took a sharp turn at the entrance to Saramount, but the gates were open and I passed through, following the driveway until the final bend brought me out onto the lawn. The house was on a point of land that curved into the river, and it seemed to follow the sweet line of that curve, gracious and elegant and starkly beautiful. Like a lady she drowsed, if a house might be likened unto a lady, wrapped in a breathless mantle of expectation, etched in silver and black, her windows dark pockets of shadows.

There were no lights, but I knew—oh yes, I knew—that Colin would be in there, and I knew in which room I would find him. Just beyond the rim of conscious thought a teasing memory tormented me, but with an effort so strong that I shook with its intensity, I throttled it down. By now, my heart was pounding so hard that it seemed the loudest sound in the world, and the breath rattled in my aching throat.

I crossed the lawn and entered by the front door, which

had been left open. Someone had thrust great trailing branches of forsythia into the umbrella stand and I heard their whisper as I brushed them in passing. I could see a flicker of light from the open door of the library and knew there must be a fire. It was there that I would find Colin waiting.

I saw him as soon as I entered. He was bent over the fireplace, resting his head on his arm. He was still wearing his navy-blue school blazer, the one he had worn when he went away, and it steamed and stank of river water, while a puddle widened on the floor around his feet. His hair, a bright flame when dry, was plastered in black streaks to his head.

"Colin," I breathed. It was just a whisper.

But he straightened, and I knew he had heard me, although he was slow in turning. And when he did, the firelight played tricks on me, with its flickering fits and starts, making pools of blackness where none existed. I thought: that is what I see, the firelight and the shadows it makes. Because his face was gone, and in its place was a skull, the flesh hanging in loathsome swollen strings from the cheekbones. He opened his mouth to speak and I saw, instead of lips, the toothy grimace of a skeleton's jaws. His eyes were cavernous pits, within their depths a dead-white mass of river amoebas, horribly, unbelievably squirming and alive.

He made a small, clacking movement toward me, and it was then that the terror, which had been building relentlessly since my nightmare began, unleashed itself and I screamed, again and again—hideous, agonizing screams, each more desperate than the one before—as though, with all hope dashed and drowned in a black darkness of despair, in that small, timeless moment between sleeping and awakening, I did not know, I could not be sure, which was real and which was the dream: the telephone call, Madeline's voice, my journey, all.

And then, like a diver rising to the surface, with arms flailing and clawing the air, I came out of that drowning darkness into sanity, to the porter's voice and a hammering on the door, while the air around me still rang and clashed with the sound of my screams.

"Miss! Miss! Is you all right?"

I could hear other voices outside my door and I realized, to my horror, that I had awakened some of my fellow passengers. I had breached the cardinal rule of Miss Warren's code: one must never, *never* make a scene. I cringed back in my berth, shaken, confused, and managed to gasp out my reassurances.

"I'm fine. I just had a nightmare. Please don't unlock the door."

There was some muttering, a laugh or two, then with a final "Yes'm," from the porter, they moved away. I knew there would be no breakfast in the morning: not for me the humiliation of facing the curious eyes in the dining car.

However, my embarrassment had no power to cast a pall over my excitement for long, now that I was awake and knew that it was all true—Colin *had* come home—and I was on my way to Saramount. I did not even waste much time on my nightmare, for it was an old one, of eleven years' duration, recurring with the persistence of a canker sore. Always the same, it had begun a year after Colin's disappearance, when the body of an adolescent boy, or young man, had floated to the surface of the river and had been accepted officially, and thereafter buried, as Colin. An impressionable seven-year-old, I had listened to some of the servants discussing the impossibility of identification after so long a time in the water. Thereafter, each night for months, I had relived the struggling horror of that confrontation with Colin as my mind remembered the vivid descriptions I had overheard. Each night I had swarmed up to wakefulness, screaming the house down, to finally fall back asleep, sobbing, in Grandfather's arms. Once, I had believed that my persistent bad dream was the reason Grandfather had sent me away to school, but it had been a long time now since I had thought that, for my nightmares had gradually subsided, even during the summers I spent at Saramount, whereas my exile at school continued. I had begged to be allowed to stay home, to attend school in nearby Charleston, as Madeline had done, but Grandfather refused point-blank, and I had never questioned his reasons. I had known he loved me and wanted me with him; children do, of course—there is a sixth sense that tells them when they are being put aside for expediency's sake. When he sent me away, it had been sorrowfully but firmly, unconditionally, and in that spirit I went.

Abner Mountain was the only guardian I had ever known, but he was not, rightfully, my grandfather. He had been—was—Colin's. I had been the interloper, resented by everyone but Grandfather and Colin, sent to live at Saramount when my parents, who were cousins, died in a malaria epidemic in Charleston. Saramount had been filled with people that summer day when I arrived, and they had all gathered around the little waif held in her nurse's arms, a frightened, panting baby of one year. A sea of strange faces, and unerringly, I had picked Colin. He had been ten years old then, and flattered and pleased to be chosen. And once made, my choice had never wavered.

That was my introduction to Saramount, and I soon learned my place there. I was not the only stray kin befriended by Grandfather. Madeline, also, had been sent to him from the Cumberlands, years before, when her parents, also distant Mountain relatives, had died, and an itinerant Methodist circuit rider had learned of her connection with Saramount and its wealthy, prominent owner, Abner Mountain.

We had been the outsiders, although we were never treated as such by Grandfather. And that summer day, when I came to Saramount, they had all been there, together, and I was easily drawn into the family circle by reason of our common ancestors, the first Abner and Sarah Mountain, who had come from England in the eighteenth century and built Saramount on the curling, shifting banks of the tawny Wando River. Rice was the money crop then: the ships left the ports in Charleston bound for England with their holds filled, and returned with fine goods and credit. The rice was grown in the savannas formed by the convergence of the two rivers, the Cooper and the Wando, and on their banks the beautiful homes sprang up and prospered. Of these, Saramount—named for a woman whose beauty was still legendary after four generations—was not only the first, but the finest.

The war changed all of that, of course: the gracious living, the plantations, the slaves whose labor made it all possible. Many of the homes were destroyed or damaged beyond repair, left to fall into neglect and decay. The Sea Island homes fared the worst, for, with their backs to the sea, abandoned by their owners who fled to Charleston, they were left wide open to marauding, roving bands that looted and burned.

Grandfather came home from that war a tired and bitter young man, to find his father and stepmother dead but, miraculously, Saramount saved for him. Taking advantage of a smallpox epidemic among the slaves, his Uncle Everard, a surgeon, had established Saramount as a hospital, for only by turning it into a charnel house could he insure that the looting troops would avoid it—literally, like a plague.

And that year, working from dawn until dark every night, Grandfather made a cotton crop at Saramount. He did it almost single-handed, with only a few doing the work that had formerly been done by a hundred, and by using his father's thoroughbred stallion, brought home riderless by his body servant, as a mule. That was the second time Saramount was saved, for the money from the cotton paid the excessive taxes levied on it. Grandfather was head of a family now, with the care of a younger half-brother and sister, the latter hardly out of the nursery herself, as well as his own wife and young son. I think he must have regretted the neglect he accorded them those first hard years, because after the deaths of his wife, then his son and daughter-in-law, he centered his love and ambition on the small grandson left him: Colin. By that time, his brother Marion had become invaluable to him, having taken over the operation of the sawmills and farmlands in order to leave Grandfather free to concentrate on what had become the pride of Saramount: the horses. Thoroughbred horses. The breeding and selling of them, and in some cases the racing of them, had become Saramount's second money-making crop. His father's stallion, which had descended in a direct line from the famous Lexington, had sired two winners, and was grandsire of a possible third.

Windsong had distinguished herself by her performance at Churchill Downs and Saratoga, but the real surprise had been Jackstraw. Tall, rangy, looking like nothing so much as an animated windmill, he had done very little to merit his training until he was about six years old. That year, he had run in a dozen handicaps and won all, galloping into the final stretches as effortlessly as though a hundred pounds of added weight was nothing.

Jackstraw was enjoying an honorable retirement in the pastures now, but his successor at Saramount had become

Traveler, who looked as though he was going to be more famous than his noble namesake. Untried as yet, he was being nursed along carefully by Victor, Uncle Marion's son, upon whose shoulders the care of the horses and Saramount had fallen, as Grandfather passed into semiretirement after Colin's disappearance. These days, Grandfather was to be found most often walking the dusty mile to the drowsy little country churchyard where most of the family was buried. Here lay the first Abner and Sarah Mountain, and here, more recently, had been placed the body of an unknown young man tentatively identified as Colin.

That year when I came to Saramount, my first, had been a sad one for the family, for the winter before, Uncle Marion and Grandfather had lost their sister, Louise. She had been a fragile, appealingly lovely young widow, with a small daughter, Rose, when she met and married the well-to-do, sophisticated Charles Manners of New York City, a man-about-town type portrayed so faithfully a few years later by Charles Dana Gibson. There also had been an aura of money about her which could not have failed to attract someone like Uncle Charles—although, to give him credit, this would not have weighed too heavily with him. He must have fallen in love, to trade so readily his much valued bachelorhood for the bonds of matrimony, however honeyed they might be.

Had Uncle Charles enjoyed his rustications in the country among his wife's relations each year? I wondered. There had been no recorded protest on his part. And they had continued after his wife's death, for though Uncle Charles had become his stepdaughter's guardian, one did not argue with Abner Mountain at his most autocratic, when he insisted that his little niece continue to pay a yearly visit to her mother's home. A very self-possessed little girl she was, this Rose, as beautiful as her mother and oddly mature for her eleven years. She never mentioned her mother, or the tragedy of losing her beneath the wheels of a runaway carriage. It was as though, in her singularly self-centered life, her mother's passing had barely stirred a ripple of change. Her days continued as before, with dancing schools and a procession of governesses and companions brought in for a carefully ordered afternoon of play. The seasonal trips to Paris or London did not change. An indulgent stepfather, who found it pleasurable to spoil her, was willingly exchanged for a frivolous mother whom she scarcely ever saw. It was only when she came home to Saramount, to be thrown into disordered conflict with her volatile Mountain cousins, that her cool composure became ruffled.

They were all about of an age, these Mountain cousins: ten-year-old Colin, eleven-year-old Rose and Madeline, and the oldest, Victor, all of twelve. I was the different one: townspeople, the family even, thought of me that way, as Sarah, the dark one. The baby with the tangled black hair and grave blue eyes. Among the others, I was distinctive, for they all possessed one characteristic in common: the red Mountain hair. Even Madeline, the distant cousin, had it. Bright auburn, crisply curling, and a direct throwback to our common ancestor, Sarah Mountain, whose portrait hung in the drawing room, and whose red hair billowed in drifts to her waist. The red-headed Mountain children—their comings and goings were watched with passionate interest by the Talley natives and reported on far and wide.

What did they say about us later, after Colin's disappearance? I wondered many times. We had continued to provide the gossips with material for speculation about Saramount and its inhabitants. Victor, to whom the fields and woods of Saramount were a religion, and who knew more about its living crop—the horses—than the heir, Colin, would have ever known, or wanted to. And Madeline, still an old maid at twenty-nine. Committed to her love for Victor. The village understood all about gentle spinsters decaying on the vine, faithful to a long-dead love for a "soldier boy" or a passing stranger. These things were not uncommon in the South. But the blazing passion that consumed Madeline, furthered by the dark hints of a shared bedroom and illicit meetings, swelled the whispers into open talk and gave the villagers cause to shoulder her aside. Even in Charleston, some of the more proper ladies inflicted snubs.

Why did they never marry? I never knew. Both were cool, self-contained people, keeping their own counsel while presenting a bland countenance to a curious society with, seemingly, no wish to legalize their love. Both had been kind, in a rather absent-minded fashion, to a younger cousin whose presence was largely ignored. Victor, I knew, was capable of much more, a fact that he openly demonstrated with only one person, his father, Uncle Marion, an invalid whom Victor tended with an agonized tenderness that was painful to watch.

But my love, my mainstay, had always been Grandfather. We comforted one another in our grief over Colin's disappearance, and long after all hope was abandoned we encouraged in each other the belief that one day he would return.

I do not know when I was told—gently, I am sure—that Colin had disappeared. Perhaps I was never really told. But I always knew. Even in the beginning, that first week or two, before the school notified Grandfather and the wheels were set in motion, I must have known. Because my grief was wild and unrestrained from the day I found him gone.

He was to go to school in Savannah, that September of

his sixteenth year, and he was excited and eager and a little scared. He had already received his school blazer, navy blue with bright silver buttons and a scarlet patch on the shoulder, and it hung proudly in his wardrobe for him to wear away, and I went into his room and glared at it a dozen times a day. He had bought his ticket on Saturday afternoon, the day before he was to leave, and his trunk had been sent on ahead then. He had gone with Grandfather to attend to those things, and I had been asked to go also, but I had stayed at home, sulking and kicking my heels against the veranda steps.

He had known that I loved him and was showing my grief in many little contrary ways, and he forgave me for every one of them, and continued to try to coax me into being happy for him. This I could not be—until that last night, when we were all leaving for the gypsy fair and I saw for myself that I was destroying my last hours with him by mourning what I could not alter.

At the fair he was kind to me, much kinder than I had a right to expect. He held me in his arms to see above the heads of the crowd when we watched the horses, and he bought and shared with me his ginger beer and taffy. When I grew tired and sleepy, he said that he was tired also, and went to Grandfather to tell him that he was taking me home. The trip did not seem so long when he allowed me to pull off my shoes and walk barefoot beside him along the dusty road in the moonlight.

He put me to bed, after dressing me in my nightgown and washing my feet and listening to my prayers, and in the doorway he paused to look at me and smiled as he said, "Goodnight, little sister."

I fell asleep, intending to use every ruse my brain could devise to delay his leavetaking the next morning, but when I came downstairs to breakfast he was gone, his valise was gone, and his bed had not been slept in. There was a certain mild puzzlement at the manner of his leaving, but nothing to alarm Grandfather until a week later, when the school notified him that although the trunk had arrived, his grandson, Colin Mountain, had not.

The search had been exhaustive. Grandfather had not stopped with officialdom; he had hired private detectives, who, with the best will in the world, had been unable to turn up any trace of a red-haired boy in a blue blazer, or indeed, any kind of boy who might remotely answer the description of Colin. The last person to admit seeing him alive was the conductor of the Midnight Limited, the train which stopped briefly in Talley before proceeding on its southwesterly course to Savannah by way of Charleston. He had punched Colin's ticket soon after pulling out of Talley, and he had recognized him the way most strangers recognized the Mountain children, by the red hair. In this case, he had also remembered the blue blazer which had been particularly Colin's. That one brief encounter was the last known sight of Colin.

It was hard to see how he could continue to be missing with all the newspaper coverage that had been given the case. There was another small flurry of publicity when a body was discovered a year later, and it was generally assumed to be Colin's. For most people, that ended the case. Grandfather accepted it as such due to pressure from the sheriff, who had wanted to write finish to an unsolved disappearance, but he had never been satisfied. And as for me, I simply refused to believe in the fact of Colin's death.

But Colin, so gentle, so good, had, by his death—or disappearance—changed the lives of us at Saramount as he never could have in life. The unexplained mystery—the crime, if it was such—had left Victor in a bitter, frustrated position that had not improved since that day. Because the first Abner Mountain was English, with English notions of inheritance, he had provided in his will that Saramount pass from eldest son to eldest son, and not be carved into small properties. The other portions of the estate—the townhouse, the mills, or any monies or lands acquired by the owner—might be divided among his heirs, but the rules regarding Saramount were rigidly observed within the family. And Saramount was what Victor wanted. Grandfather could have broken the impasse by legal means, but he could not bring himself to the finality of acknowledging Colin's death. So he vacillated, leaving Victor in an untenable position, not knowing if what he brooded over with such passionate intensity was to be his, or if he was merely carefully husbanding it for the future of another owner who might appear anytime and demand his rights.

Victor's life had perhaps been blighted even more than mine by those unaccountable events of that September twelve years ago, for at some time during Grandfather's stay in Savannah, Uncle Marion had suffered a stroke, changing him from a vigorous, active man into a helpless invalid.

As for Rose and her stepfather, Uncle Charles, who had been dawdling through the summer at Saramount, they, too, felt the impact of the changed circumstances. Plans were already firm that they were to leave in a day or two for New York, and they were gone before the dreadful tidings from Savannah came to us. But they had never been back: whose decision, Grandfather did not know, but he had not had the heart to insist that they change it. All was different, all was unhappy: how could he do so?

So life went on, but not the same. Never the same. And though months, and then years, went by, when his name was hardly mentioned by anyone but Grandfather and me —and then only in the privacy of our moments together—

Colin was uppermost in everyone's thoughts. He lived with us constantly a young, diffident, sweet-natured boy who could never be mourned in peace.

And now, he was back. I had Madeline's word for that. It was not just another dream created from the imagination of a desperately lonely child. Colin was back, and whatever else his coming might bring, life at Saramount was changed. Permanently. And once again, nothing would ever be the same.

CHAPTER 2

Overnight the wind had changed its course: it was blowing from the south and I could smell the sea. Last night darkness had fallen on the mountains, forested with the towering spruce trees, the oak and the hickory. This morning I had awakened to a dramatic change in the landscape. For the past hour the train had rumbled over trestles built over low-lying swamps, and followed tracks cutting through pine flats and small, dusty, lowland villages. The rhododendron and the laurel, the columbine and the snowy trillium covering the mountainside had given way to a new scene— deeper, softer, more lush and in some subtle way, more enticing. Boggy bays, carpeted with rotting moss and great pads of yellow lotus and hibiscus, encircled and concealed the bell bottoms of the black gums and the cypress trees that waded in the black waters of the swamp. Behind me lay the midlands: the wide, rolling sandhills of the old beaches and dunes of a long-receded sea. Ahead was the ocean, restless and vibrantly alive. And Saramount.

It was a change that I never tired watching unfold, and it had never failed yet to work its miracle. Already I felt the magic of coming home. Like a dog with his nose to the scent, I sniffed the air eagerly as the scrub loblolly pine flashed past my window. Suddenly a flock of white heron, startled by the noise of the train, arose from where they had been feeding, wheeling and dipping in ungainly flight, and I laughed aloud at their awkwardness and with the sheer joy of knowing I was near my journey's end, that I had left behind me the dreary rain of yesterday, and with it, my fears and bad dreams.

Not even the cautious look directed at me by the porter when he entered to fold my bed, dimmed my high spirits, although I had not had the courage to face the curious occupants of the dining car.

As though to point up even further the absurdity of my nightmare, the reality of my arrival was attended by all the bright afternoon sunlight and frenzied activity that it had lacked. I was assisted from the train by the porter, clearly relieved to be rid of his charge, and as I stood hesitating beside my trunk, was aware of more than one speculative look directed my way by the knot of idlers who were accustomed to sit about the platform and watch the train come in. Such covert curiosity could mean only one thing. The word was out—Colin was home—and a crowd had gathered to see if anything could be learned from my reaction. I looked over their heads and saw Shand, waiting beside the buggy which had been parked beneath a grove of trees near the platform.

He came forward, tugging at his straw-hat brim, and without a word, took my trunk and valise, then settled me on the buggy seat. I knew that he had already been subjected to a cross-examination, and I respected his silence. As he swung the buggy in a wide arc around the watering trough in the center of the square, he was forced to make way for a shambling, stumbling figure that stepped into our path and flagged us to a halt. It was Joe Bob Harrison, the town drunk, onetime childhood playmate of Colin's and, therefore, mine.

"Did you know that Colin was back, Sarah?"

"Yes, Joe Bob. That's why I'm home," I answered gently.

For once he was sober, cold sober, an apt enough phrase considering the shivering effort it was costing him. He was blinking in the hot sunlight and kept fingering his unshaven chin, while he steadied himself by leaning against the side of the buggy.

"The news is all over town, Sarah. I heard all about it the first time at the general store. Have you seen him yet?"

"Not yet, Joe Bob. I just arrived. I'll tell Colin you were asking about him," I added soothingly.

"No!" He shook his head violently. "That's not what I want. Stop trying to put me off," he added disconcertingly. "I have to see him, Sarah. I *must* see him! You tell him that. Tell him to meet me at the Old Place. He'll remember. It's important now. You mind me, Sarah?"

"I mind you, Joe Bob." I pulled my skirts free from his clutching fingers. "I have to go now."

"You don't understand how important it is," he repeated desperately. "I must see him. I guess I have heard the whole story a dozen times, now, since he got back. It's all over town."

Poor Joe Bob, once he got hold of the end of a stick, he never let go, I thought pityingly. How many times must he repeat himself before he released the shaking hold he had on the buggy? Once he had been the darling of his mother's heart, but without that same mother to cry over him, who cared now that he drank himself insensible each night?

I could understand how he had indeed "heard the whole story a dozen times," for Colin's reappearance would be the talk of Talley. His disappearance, with all its novelistic ingredients—the missing heir, the midnight train journey, the floating body—had been Talley's own mystery, to which they could point with pride and awe. Now the return of Colin would bring the little village once more into the light. The story would provide talk for the citizenry to chew over for years to come. The Mountains of Saramount had never failed them yet, when it came to providing entertainment.

Shand was muttering, so with another promise I managed to rid myself of Joe Bob. When we were out of earshot, Shand protested openly.

"Ain't seemly fo' you to hold conversation wit' thet Joe Bob Harrison in th' middle of th' street, Miz Sarey. He mebbee harmless, but he long time ago disgrace hisself by gittin' to be th' town drunk."

I shrugged, dismissing Joe Bob from my mind. "Has Colin changed much, Shand?" I asked eagerly.

"Yo' gran'pap doan' think so."

"What about you? What do you think?"

"It doan' mattah what Ah think—Ah ain't th' one to be reckoned wit'."

I studied the back of his woolly gray head and the wrinkled black hands holding the reins. For the first time, I found myself seriously wondering what the others would think of Colin's return. I had been filled with excitement and anticipation to the exclusion of all else, but obviously not everyone would have the same reaction. What about Victor? His circumstances were changed now. Would he marry Madeline now that, at long last, he knew what his future would be? And Uncle Marion and Aunt Lucy? After Grandfather's death, would there be a place for them at Saramount with Colin as its master? The questions surged into my mind, one after another, providing me with no answers, since I had been given no clues from the scant information I had. I probed, tentatively.

"What do you really think about him, Shand? Is he like himself?"

"As to thet, Miz Sarey, Ah cain't say. You know, us nevah know much 'bout Mistah Colin. He nevah was int'rested much in th' horses, lak Mistah Victah was, from th' time he's a leetle boy. Now, though, he *mighty* int'rested!" Shand's voice was dry. "He all ovah Traveler!" he added scornfully. "Jes lak he bred him, heself! Jes seem t'me an' th' rest of us, it *mighty* hard on Mistah Victah, aftah all these yeahs."

Well, I had my answer. Of course, Shand would be loyal to Victor. He had been born at Saramount. He had married Paulie, my nurse, who had brought me from Charleston seventeen years ago, and if Shand had an opinion, it meant that it was shared by most of the other servants. Victor would not have to ask for their support; it would be given as naturally as they breathed the air of Saramount, because he had been the natural successor to Grandfather. He had been involved in, and concerned with, their interests and problems. Why wouldn't they repay him with a loyalty they could no longer give to Grandfather, and, certainly, never to Colin? For years, now, Victor had been the master of Saramount in all but name. The buying trips, the auctions, the shows had been his responsibility. And now, Traveler. The finest racehorse yet to be produced by the stables of Saramount. Victor had been excited and ambitious for him. Was this, too, to be Colin's victory?

I had let myself forget Madeline's last words, but they returned now with greater emphasis: "Victor thinks he is an impostor." It would, of course, be to his advantage to throw doubt on Colin's identity, but I couldn't see how it would be possible to seriously question it, since, apparently, Grandfather did not.

I said no more to Shand. The very set of his shoulders discouraged conversation. Ordinarily, he was as garrulous as an old woman, eager to be the first to tell me the news on my homeward drive from the station each spring. But things were different now. Sides had been drawn, and

Shand had planted himself squarely on Victor's; and until I proved myself, he was giving nothing more away.

We were not long in arriving, riding in almost total silence, broken by the clop of the horses' hooves as they beat the hard-packed shell road. At the gate, the road veered sharply at right angles to meander for miles along the property line of Saramount's woods, but the drive tunneled for another half mile beneath massive, overhanging trees, dripping with the gray-green fronds of Spanish moss, before ending in a wide circle in front of the house. Flowering dogwood and red buds glinted in the cleared openings between the trees, and masses of brilliant red and white azaleas were banked against the house. At the corner of the summer kitchen, a wisteria vine blossomed in a cloud of mauve and pink. The rosy old bricks of Saramount seemed to take on an extra glow from the reflected glory of all the color.

I was pale and shaking with nervousness, and Shand, seeing my pallor, permitted a small smile to tug at the corner of his mouth as he pulled up beneath the porte cochere.

"Mistah Abnah'll be in the liberry, Miz Sarey," he explained kindly. "You go on in an' Ah'll unload yo' things."

I didn't wait. My feet flew across the veranda and in through the open door. As always, when entering the house, one's eyes were drawn to the circular stairway that dominated the front hall. Gracefully curving upward, dark oak and creamy white, its black cypress railing had known the hands of generations of Saramount's occupants, and the steps had been worn to a sunken groove by their feet. Unfamiliar though I was with the housekeeping arrangements, I nevertheless recognized signs that all had been recently refurbished. The chandelier sparkled from a thorough cleaning with soap and water, and the silk wallpaper, brought over long ago from England in a four-masted

sailing vessel, and since hoarded carefully, had been recently cleaned. Everywhere there was an abundance of
flowers. I knew that none of this had been done for my
benefit, and concluded it must have been for Colin and our
house guests, as well as the eyes of the curious callers we
could begin to expect soon.

No one came forward to greet me, allowing me to find
my way to Grandfather alone. The library was normally a
dark room when the broad limbs of the giant oaks spotting
the south lawn were in full leaf, but today it was filled with
light and warmth from the open, floor-length windows.
Bands of sunlight lay across the floor, illuminating the
shabby, comfortable old furniture and the worn red carpet.
Two people were seated in soft leather armchairs, obviously deep in conversation. Grandfather and Colin. They
both looked up, blinking, as I paused in the doorway, and
then Grandfather smiled and held out his hand as Colin
rose slowly to his feet, watching me warily.

He was tall and strongly built, and I knew him at once
by his resemblance to Victor and Grandfather. His broad,
muscular shoulders and powerful frame gave the impression of a man who has spent his life out of doors. Even in
the midst of my painful joy and excitement, I had a moment of wonder at how he had changed, for Colin had been
a thin, ascetic boy who had wanted to be a doctor. But this
was merely a passing thought, as fleet as the breeze that
stirred his hair. Mountain hair. Red, russet red, and crisply
curling, topping a weathered, craggily good-looking face,
with well-shaped lips quirked in a tentative little smile, and
brown eyes that gradually lost their wariness to change to
amusement as he assessed my emotions.

It was the hair that did it, of course. The red Mountain
hair. It, and it alone, meant Colin to me. Without a mo-

ment's pause to stop and consider, I launched myself straight into his arms.

He was taken aback. I felt his shock as he stiffened, and his hesitation before he tentatively clasped his arms about my waist. I looked up and saw Colin smiling at me, tender, rather amused, and I pulled his face down and covered it with kisses. This time there was no hesitation, but it was a minute before I became aware that my greedy, impetuous kisses were being returned. Quite leisurely—and yet, in a manner that was unmistakable—he had tightened his grip, and the next kiss that landed by accident on his lips was prolonged and warmly, exploratively, answered. I jerked back, my face flaming, to look directly into his eyes. There was an ironic glint in them as he loosened his grasp on my waist with deliberate slowness.

I tried desperately to remember that this tall, cool stranger was Colin, but, alarmingly, I could only see juxtaposed upon his features the gentle, childish ones of the boy I remembered.

"Grandfather," I called imploringly, reaching desperately for a lifeline as I felt consciousness slip away, and the arms that had been reluctantly withdrawing tightened again as I knew nothing more.

I came to myself while Colin was lowering me into his chair. Grandfather was bent over me, chafing my hands.

"Some brandy," he was saying. "She has had a shock."

"Grandfather," I whispered, but he hushed me.

"Don't try to talk yet, honey, until you've had some brandy. You've had quite a shock. I blame myself, for I should've known this would happen. You've waited too long for this moment."

"Yes," I agreed tiredly and closed my eyes. I opened them a moment later, to interrupt a look between Colin and Grandfather, a knowing look, with Colin raising a questioning eyebrow and Grandfather replying with a slight pursing of his lips. Colin shrugged and pressed a glass to my lips. Obediently I drank, and the brandy almost instantly did its work and steadied me.

"Are you feeling better, child?"

"Yes, thank you, Grandfather." I was sitting up straight now and carefully not looking at Colin, although I was intensely aware that he was leaning against the table, his long legs crossed, while he watched me steadily.

"Well, Sarah, am I what you expected?" he asked.

I jumped. His voice was shockingly unfamiliar, even allowing for the deepening tones of maturity. I frowned slightly, unable to explain its unexpectedness.

Before I could reply, Grandfather interposed gently, as though aware of my confusion. "Sarah has had a shock, Sister. I think you should take her upstairs and put her to rest for the afternoon."

Madeline was standing in the doorway, and the change in her made me blink. She had always had a great potential for beauty, which she had deliberately drabbed with indifferent clothes and an unbecoming hairstyle. One seldom saw her in anything other than riding clothes or tailored suits, with her hair pulled severely away from her face. Tall, stately, with that unblemished milk-white complexion that sometimes goes with red hair, she was in flawless form atop a hunter, dressed in one of the well-tailored riding habits she favored. But there was no place for a riding crop and boots in a drawing room, and I had come to believe that Madeline's nature would not allow her to clad herself in clothes that were soft and feminine. Now, dressed in something clinging with ruffles, her hair a swirl of red curls around her face, the improvement was remarkable, although the ironic expression in her eyes, as she regarded me, was unchanged.

"I am sure you want to wash up, Sarah. Come along."

Until then, I had not been conscious of my grubbiness, or the specks of coal dust sprinkling my shirtwaist and, I suspected, my face. I stood up hurriedly and Colin straightened himself slowly.

"You haven't answered my question, Sarah. Have I changed?"

"I suppose so," I said hesitantly, "although I would have known you anywhere. You look like Victor."

"And Victor and Colin looked alike as boys," Grandfather said firmly. "Colin only has to stand under the family portraits for us to see the resemblance."

Of course. That was it. The Mountain clan was distinctive with their red hair, bony noses and craggy jaws, features that continued to crop up again and again in its male members. One could trace it in the family portraits as it leapfrogged among the generations. Not always did those characteristic features run true, however, for they had bypassed their fathers to touch Victor, Abner and Colin Mountain. Or was that what it was? Were they, then, a type: a type that because of its very individuality, might resemble a total stranger more than a close relative?

I wasn't aware that I was staring at Colin until Grandfather murmured, "Poor Sarah. Child, don't try to think about it now. Go upstairs and rest—you've had a difficult day."

"Yes," Colin agreed absently.

I turned away with another look at my dirty hands and followed Madeline upstairs. We were in the doorway of my room when the little memory that had been teasing me surfaced to the top layer of my mind.

"Sister! I know what was wrong with Colin's voice! He spoke with an English accent!"

She paused to give me a pitying look before pushing me

inside. "Of course. It will all be explained to you later, Sarah. Grandfather asked me to wait until Colin can tell you and Uncle Charles about it himself."

"But *you* know why?"

"Naturally. I have heard his story. He has been here a week, you know, and I've had time to discuss it thoroughly with him." She shut the door firmly behind me. "I might as well tell you, Sarah, it gets stranger with every telling, but he has Grandfather absolutely convinced that he is Colin, and you know how immovable Grandfather can be."

"But how can there be any doubt?" I asked, puzzled. "He looks like Colin would look, and surely, any of you can question him about his memories."

She stood at my dressing table, her back turned to me. Apparently, someone had already unpacked my valise, and now she played nervously with my comb and brush and refused to meet my eyes in the mirror. "Oh, yes, we have questioned him, all right. And he knows most of the answers. But there are gaps. Things he doesn't remember. But I won't go into that now."

"You can at least tell me how he came here," I pleaded, sinking onto my bed and gripping the post with both hands. "Did he just appear one day and say, 'Here I am'?"

She turned, relieved to be on firmer ground. "Oh, yes, I can tell you that. He wrote Grandfather a letter from the St. John Hotel in Charleston. He had been in town a week, he said, trying to get up the courage to come home, and he wanted to know if Grandfather wanted him back. Naturally, as soon as he received the letter, that same day, Grandfather went to Charleston and returned with him. He was already firmly convinced that he was Colin by the time they got home."

"Did Colin say why he stayed away so long?"

She shrugged, as though already losing interest in the

conversation. "Oh, he has an explanation for everything. But there is no way to really prove who he is. Colin had no birthmark, no identifying scars—"

Now it was my turn to feel superior. "That sort of thing occurs only in books, Sister, and it's absurd to expect real life to be like a fairy tale. We all remember Colin too well; we only have to question him. I, for one, couldn't be fooled by an impostor."

She laughed. "Oh, Sarah, you would be the first one fooled. You were only a baby when he left and your memories are indistinct at best. And if those kisses are an indication, you are already convinced."

I flushed scarlet, ashamed that she had witnessed my unrestrained greeting, but she scarcely heeded my confusion. Something was bothering Madeline. She was restless and I sensed an evasiveness behind her seeming frankness. Instead of following up her devastating comment, as the old Madeline would have delighted doing, she moved over to my window and stood staring blindly down upon the lawn. I watched her hopefully, uncomfortably aware of my unwashed body and empty stomach, yet hesitant to remind her of the courtesies she would have automatically extended to a guest.

"You mentioned Uncle Charles," I said cautiously. "Is he here already?"

"Yes, he arrived last night and is still resting," she replied absently. "We'll see what he makes of this—this Colin. He is a cool observer and he has no axe to grind." She looked up and flushed as she met my eyes. "Oh, I know what you're thinking," she cried. "That Victor has persuaded me into his way of thinking. But I am keeping an open mind, for if this man *is* Colin, I would be the first to want to know the truth about what happened to him!" Her eyes grew more intent and she stared, as though seeing me for the first time. "Sarah, *where* did you get those clothes?" she demanded.

"What's wrong with them?" I asked sullenly. I had been proud of my new long skirt, but her curt question made me look at it with awakened eyes. The two large pins I had used to anchor my white shirtwaist had tugged loose, allowing my navy serge skirt, unsuitably hot for the humid climate, to ruck sideways. "After all, I only went into long skirts this winter, and Miss Warren—"

"Miss Warren was a dowd, and the clothes she chose for you reflect her tastes. You are no longer at school, Sarah, and you will do well to forget some of the things you learned there. Certainly, about fashion. Your clothes are a disgrace." By this time, Madeline was on her knees before my trunk, flinging out my school uniforms to lie, shamefully exposed in all their unfashionable drabness, on the bed. "Navy-blue skirts and white waists, and every one full of holes from those safety pins you use. Can't you keep yourself tucked in any other way? Nothing here is suitable for summer!"

I thought resentfully that on the basis of a few new clothes of her own, Madeline was hardly qualified as an expert. She had never before cared how I dressed, and I didn't hesitate to say as much to her.

"Try to remember that you are no longer twelve years old, Sarah," she answered crushingly. "And be thankful that I am willing to take the time to get you something new. I simply don't intend to have Rose arrive here with her Paris clothes and look down her nose at us."

"Oh." Could this be the reason for the change in Madeline? "I do appreciate it, Sister," I said humbly.

"You're too small to wear any of my things," she went on. "I had two cotton frocks made up for you by a Charleston dressmaker last week, and tomorrow we shall go for a fitting on some other garments. You don't remember Rose," she added, "but I do very well. She had a way of making one feel—inadequate. And unwanted. After all, you and I have no real place here. We are merely distant kin, and she is Grandfather's own niece. When I was a child I once heard her asking Grandfather to send us both away."

I was shocked. "But he would never do that! He's our grandfather."

"Don't be childish, Sarah," Madeline said crisply, rising to her feet and gathering my despised shirtwaists in her arms. "He is *not* our grandfather. He is Colin's grandfather, and we have no claim on him. I warn you right now, my girl, this situation may be dangerous. Unless Rose has changed, she won't like either of us, and she may decide that we have battened on Grandfather long enough and that it is time for us to move on. She used to be able to twist Grandfather around her little finger, just as she does Uncle Charles, and she may still be able to do so. And with Colin home, we don't know what may happen. Colin has never married; neither has Rose—and you know that cousins wed frequently to keep big fortunes in the family. Grandfather would love to see things tied up neatly that way."

My heart felt drained of its blood, and I knew my face had whitened at the implication of her words. "Colin—and Rose?" I asked bewilderedly.

"Exactly. I think it is rather significant that Grandfather is insisting that she return. He gives as his excuse that he wants her opinion on Colin; but actually, he needs only Uncle Charles for that. I believe he has another purpose in bringing her here, and that is—he wants to tie Colin securely to Saramount with a wife, so he won't be tempted to leave again." Madeline's thin, arrogant face had sharpened to a point.

"Grandfather would never send me away," I whispered, harking back to her earlier words.

A flicker of impatience crossed her face. "He has been sending you away with regularity since you were eight years old!" she snapped. "He has educated you—he owes you nothing more! Hasn't what I said made any impression? Colin is back and changes will be made!"

I didn't answer her, and my face must have mirrored my shock, for, with an irritable snort, as though dismissing me as an unworthy ally, Madeline turned away impatiently. "Never mind, Sarah. First things first. I'll take these things to Paulie to be mended."

But I stopped her at the door with a timid request for food and, spurred by her obvious astonishment, found myself stumbling through a laborious explanation of why I had missed breakfast and lunch. She interrupted me before I had gotten halfway through my narrative.

"That's enough, Sarah," she said witheringly. "I understand that you allowed yourself to be misled into thinking that a dining car full of total strangers would observe you merely because you awakened screaming from a bad dream the night before. For that, you did without two meals and, no doubt, thereby made yourself even more conspicuous to the porter and the conductor. It's not important, however. I'll bring you a tray."

Apparently, Madeline remembered nothing of the nightmares that had turned me, overnight, into a shaking, little, troubled shadow of my former lighthearted self. Of course, she had been an adolescent girl at the time, heedless of whatever did not directly concern herself, but I had assumed that something so searingly prominent in my own memory would have been retained to a lesser degree by the others. My life had been torn asunder by the onset of the nightmares so that I had gradually come to view them with a great deal of superstitious dread, yet, seemingly, they had made no impression on the occupants of Saramount, just as my coming and going had scarcely made a ripple in their lives. Sitting alone at my scrubbed little oak desk, eating my dinner from a tray, I gazed thoughtfully about my room, seeing it for the first time with adult eyes. My collection of dolls still occupied the window seat, and lambs and bunnies gamboled in a never-ending game of leapfrog across the coverlet and hangings of my bed. It had remained untouched and childish, just as it was when I was eight years old, as though with each September, when I pulled the door shut, the room and I were both forgotten until I returned in the spring.

Well—no more, I thought grimly. I would cling like a burr to Saramount this time, and it would take the combined efforts of Rose, Colin and, yes, even Grandfather himself, to dislodge me.

Paulie had brought out my hip bath, which had been reposing modestly behind a screen in the corner, and filled it with hot water so that I could wash away the train cinders and travel dust before I rested, but in my new stubborn mood, I had no intention of meekly retiring to bed. My eyes fell on the two dresses Madeline had left for me. They were pastels, colors suitable for a young girl, with round collars and short, capelike sleeves. To my inexperienced eyes, however, there was nothing childish about the simple little cotton dress which, when I put it on, swished satisfyingly about my feet. My pier glass showed me a rounded young girl, shorter than the currently popular, tall, swanlike American Beauty rose, and a far cry from Madeline's proud height. I had attempted to rectify my lack of inches by piling my thick, heavy hair atop my head, à la

Gibson Girl, but my little gamine face was not the Gibson Girl type, nor were my sooty blue eyes. However, as I eyed myself in the mirror, I noticed smugly that the dress revealed curves that had nothing to do with childishness.

I found Grandfather alone in the library, bent over the table as he filled his pipe from the humidor, and I watched him for a moment, unseen. Grandfather had aged more than his allotted years in the decade since Colin's disappearance. His hair, springing from a broad, high forehead, was still thick, but its former grizzled auburn had whitened. There were deeply engraved lines above the high, arched nose, and his frail, blue-veined hands shook slightly as he packed the tobacco into his pipe. My heart swelled with love as I watched him. Unlike Madeline, I had never needed reassurance about my position at Saramount. Grandfather not love me! *Never!* But it was true that I had never pulled my weight here. Other than being Grandfather's pet, I had had no role to play, and if Saramount underwent an upheaval, how long would that last?

I stirred, and Grandfather looked up with a smile.

"A vast improvement over the school uniform," he teased gently as he held out his arms.

I came forward and laid my cheek against his. "Grandfather," I whispered, "do you want me here? Are you glad I am home?"

He was very still for a moment, then drew back and looked at me reproachfully. "What's this? You can't be jealous of Colin? Not my Sarah?"

"Oh, no, Grandfather, not of Colin! Never of Colin! But —but—you haven't wanted me home for all these years. You—you—have sent me away to—school—" I halted to a stammering stop.

He sat down in his big armchair and drew me to his lap. He said nothing for a minute, then stirred and sighed. "Because of the nightmares, Sarah. The doctor told me you would lose your reason if they continued in their intensity. You have always felt things so much, Sarah."

"But I don't have nightmares now," I persisted. "I haven't had them for a long time. Yet, I—I—have had to stay away at school."

He smiled and pinched my cheek, but I did not misunderstand the deft way he ignored my question and changed the subject. "Now that you are putting up your hair and wearing long skirts, I expect those nightmares to change to dreams of parties and beaux. In the future, I look for a swarm of young men to be always at our door, and I intend to question each and every one as to his intentions!"

I relaxed, lulled into indiscretion by the rich, beloved accents. "Ah, Grandfather," I chided, "you know that Colin is the only beau I have ever wanted!"

That it was an indiscretion I knew at once by the way he stiffened, the smile leaving his face as though wiped off a slate. "No, Sarah, Colin is not for you. He's had ten years' hard living behind him and you could never span the gap that exists between you two now. Your life is ahead of you, and it's a full, exciting life, with your debut at St. Cecelia's Ball, and all the parties and pretty frocks that go with that, including romantic young men serenading you in the moonlight. No, no, my child, I don't want you to forego all that because of some childish notion about Colin. Forget him."

I was equally embarrassed and hurt. True, I had been joking when I called Colin my beau, but Grandfather would understand how serious that joke was. He had always known how I felt about Colin, and I, in turn, had heard him say many times that his cherished ambition was that we would someday marry, yet now he was sternly forbidding it. Had I erred in not listening to Madeline? Could

Grandfather be thinking of Colin and Rose, who was in every way a perfect wife for him, a perfect mistress of Saramount? How could I have doubted Madeline, who had had a week to understand Grandfather's plans for Colin's future?

He was looking at me anxiously. "Sarah," he asked worriedly, "you do understand, don't you? Colin may be an impostor, or worse, and I—I can't allow you to fall in love with him, child." He added diffidently, "We must make sure of his identity before we accept him wholeheartedly into the family, and I wouldn't want you to be hurt, my darling."

I reared back and stared at him in astonishment. "But Madeline said—"

"Yes, I can imagine what Madeline said." He smiled ruefully. "That I was convinced of Colin's truthfulness? Well, why not? If he is really my boy, I would not want to insult him by allowing him to see any doubts. And also," he added with an engaging little twinkle, "I know that Victor will work that much harder to prove his identity, if he feels that he has to convince me."

Why, the wily old fox! Remembering Madeline's absolute conviction, I gazed at him admiringly. He had fooled them all, but I wondered if he had fooled Colin. Remembering, a shadow touched my heart, even as it passed over my face. "Grandfather," I said hesitantly, "if he *isn't* Colin—"

"Yes, I know," he said gently. "If he isn't, then we are right back where we started, with our hearts broken. But perhaps a bit closer to the truth," he added grimly, "for if he is an impostor, that means he has assistance from someone who is playing a game with us, and I will be very, very interested in finding out who that person is, and his motive."

I shivered, feeling a little daunted. How simple it had seemed last night, but if Grandfather was still a doubter, then I must keep my wits about me as I talked to Colin and try to discover the truth for myself. Apparently, there were small incongruities in his story, but were they important ones, or merely the sort that the fading memory of an adolescent boy might produce?

Tea was early, ordered by Grandfather particularly so that Uncle Charles and I might have no delay in hearing Colin's story. Like a child being granted a treat after a disappointment, he asked me to preside behind the tray and pour.

Nathan followed Colin into the library, trundling the tea cart, and promptly destroyed the impression of maturity I was seeking to advance. With the freedom of an old servant, he admonished me to be careful with the boiling water, and added that the stickies were fresh and sent from the kitchen by Mammy, since she knew they were favorites of mine, but that I must not make myself sick by overeating the rich little cookies. Nathan was exactly Grandfather's age, they had been childhood playmates, they had gone to war together and returned together to face a devastated Saramount. Nathan carried himself with the same military erectness as Grandfather, even though his hair had, if anything, whitened more, and his hands trembled slightly as he passed the teacups. I noticed him watching Grandfather anxiously as he fussed about the room, closing the open windows and scolding about the noxious effect of fresh air on elderly throats.

"You worry about your own throat, Nate, and let me worry about mine," Grandfather said good-humoredly. "The ev'ning air at Saramount hasn't killed me yet, and I've got a while to go."

Nathan pursed his lips but was prevented from replying

by the unusual arrival of Madeline and Victor together. It was not a habit of theirs to drink afternoon tea with the family. Normally, Victor worked in the stables and Madeline took it to him there and remained with him while he drank it, black and hot out of a thick china mug, while they talked of horses and rotating crops. Victor was not inclined to indulge in small talk, and I knew he regarded the ritual of afternoon tea as suitable only for idle women, dilettantes and elderly folk. Therefore, his appearance was something of a surprise, particularly since he had also made the concession of doffing his stable clothes for a white shirt and tie, with neatly pressed cotton breeches thrust into boots that had been scraped clean of stable mire and polished for the occasion.

Now that both were together, I could see that Victor was slightly taller and broader of shoulder than Colin, but their craggy faces and high arched noses were strikingly similar. Both wore the fashionably long sideburns and flowing hairstyle of the day, which served to increase their resemblance.

Just behind Madeline and Victor was Uncle Charles. I had not seen him for twelve years, but I remembered him as a gay, delightful, fun-loving man who kept candies in his pocket and encouraged me to climb into his lap while he told me stories. But where had he gone? Who was this stooped, aging man with the lost eyes? Dull, dead, dispirited, they reminded me of those in the pictures I had seen of statues found on the hillsides of Greece. Lusterless eyes, lacking emotion, vision, and more particularly, life itself. On this hopeless face, his once suave good looks sat oddly, quenched to a ghastly parody. Was Rose responsible for this alteration in her stepfather?

He greeted me with charming courtesy before seating himself, demonstrating that his manners, at least, had not undergone a change.

"What did you bring *him* down for?" Victor rasped violently. Aunt Lucy was wheeling her husband into the room in his chair. With their coming, our little group was complete.

"He wanted to come," she said defiantly to her son.

"I don't believe it," he snarled savagely. "You did it deliberately, in order to force me to—" With an effort so visible that one could see the muscles bunch in his jaws, he throttled the remainder of his sentence.

"That's enough, Victor," Grandfather said sternly. "Your father enjoys being with people, and he shall stay."

I rose and went over to kiss Uncle Marion's cheek. He had understood his son's boorishness and his eyes were filmy with tears in the frozen face. His hands, working free of the blanket, wriggled toward mine.

"Would you like some tea?"

He made no attempt to speak, something he could partially do only after a long, agonizing struggle, but he slowly lowered his eyelids once, a signal that he and I had worked out as "No" long ago, when I was a child. I nodded and pulled my chair close to his. I had been one of the few people with whom he could communicate since his stroke. Before that fateful time, I have a singularly blank memory of him; he apparently faded into insignificance beside the more forceful personalities of his elder brother and his son. That first winter, when he was allowed to be up, he would be wheeled to the veranda to sit in the sun, and often I played nearby with my dolls. It seemed to soothe him to watch me. The day they discovered me in his resistless lap reading to him from my book, they were horrified and attempted to take him away, only to discover that he fought like a silent tiger to be allowed to remain. He seemed to enjoy my company, and my presence could usually quiet the restless hands and soothe the taut, strained face.

Victor's outburst could be partially explained by the fact that his father normally had his meals in his room and was fed by his valet. If, as he had intimated, his mother had brought him down for some purpose, I knew it would not be a humane one, for her dislike and contempt for the man whose name she bore was equaled by her possessive love for her son. My memories of her, unlike her husband, were filled with fear and revulsion. She was a tall, strong-looking woman of plain countenance, with jet-black hair which, I once discovered, was ink-dyed. Innocently repeating my discovery to a giggling Madeline, who promptly made it public, taught me a healthy respect for Aunt Lucy's temper and a wish to never incur it again.

"Well, Sarah, what do you think of our alleged cousin? Or, are you already convinced, as Madeline seems to think, that he is the real Colin?" Victor was watching Colin, a challenging look in his eyes.

"Do you mean that you doubt him?" Uncle Charles was surprised. "Is this what all of you think?" He looked questioningly at Grandfather.

"Victor alone is vocal about his doubts," Grandfather replied evasively.

"With a property like Saramount involved," Victor said shortly, "it would be foolish to take the word of a total stranger who walks in and claims to be the long-lost heir, without checking his story."

The mystery of Victor's appearance was explained—he was unable to hide his aggressiveness for long. He had flung the gauntlet at Colin, who was making no attempt to pick it up. Instead, he seemed more concerned with whispering secrets in Madeline's ear. When she laughed, Victor flushed.

"My dear boy"—Uncle Charles was reproachful—"he is hardly a total stranger. He is Colin. Look at his resemblance to the rest of you. To claim otherwise is ridiculous. Surely his identity can be cleared up easily—in fact, has already been. He was—what?—sixteen when he left home. We all remember him too well. A few questions should straighten this out immediately."

"That is just the point, Charles," Grandfather explained. "Colin has answered all—or most—of our questions correctly, but he has one large gap in his memory. Because of that, Victor continues to doubt his claim."

"Victor, old chap—" Uncle Charles began.

"He is not Colin!" Victor interrupted angrily. "He is an impostor! A clever one, I grant you that, but nevertheless, he is not my cousin Colin. He knows some things—but they are things any knowledgeable person could have told him. Bah! What is that? Colin and I were close—we shared many experiences no one else would know; but he doesn't speak of, or seem to remember, those! I would like to get the opinion of someone like Joe Bob, who—"

I was reminded of my encounter today. "Joe Bob wants to see you," I said eagerly, addressing Colin. "I saw him at the station and he asked—"

"Yes, Nate had to send him packing when he came to the door drunk," Grandfather interrupted, then added curiously, "Do you mean he was sober today?"

"And obviously a phenomenon thereby," drawled Colin. "From what I have heard, he is seldom making sense. I would not like to be the subject of his maudlin recollections. No, Victor, I would like to oblige, but my confrontation with Joe Bob will have to wait."

"It wasn't that way—" I began, but no one was listening to me, least of all Victor, who had already discarded Joe Bob as a subject.

"You have become adept at avoiding any confrontation that might embarrass you," he was saying, "and apparently, you have Uncle Abner on your side, so long as you maintain a plausible reason for doing so!"

Colin flushed angrily, and I wondered at his forbearance, but more, particularly, at Grandfather's. Once he would have made quick work of Victor's sneers and disrespect, but instead, he sat huddled in his armchair and was silent while Victor made the rude noises of a fractious child. Was he growing old and weak, like his brother? It was left for Uncle Charles to soothe the stormy atmosphere by tactfully asking Colin to explain what had happened to him after he left Saramount twelve years ago, for "I confess to a great deal of curiosity, myself."

As soon as Colin began to speak, I saw why Victor was balking at his identity. Colin had no explanation for what had happened to him. He remembered the gypsy fair, he said, and the earlier events of that night. The children had walked together to the fair, while the adults had ridden in the buggy. Once there, we had separated, or paired off, and I was left as Colin's charge. He remembered the things we had done and seen: the gypsy fortune-teller, the sword swallower, and most importantly, the horses, to be auctioned from a ring in the center of the crowd. Stolen, perhaps, but of blood stock. And the sturdy little ponies for the children, with their shaggy manes and soft, liquid eyes. Yes, he remembered and, as he talked, I remembered too. Victor's face grew more sour, and I knew that Colin's account of people whom he had seen and spoken to had already been investigated. "About the remainder of the evening," he added, "I am blank. I know I left with Sarah, but beyond that—nothing. I am hoping that she and I, together, can go over the details of that night until she can come up with something that will prod my memory—or hers."

I blinked at him, intrigued by the possibility. Victor snorted.

"What is your next recollection?" Uncle Charles asked hastily, with a reproachful look at Victor.

"The following afternoon, in Savannah. I awakened with a loss of memory, a pounding headache, and a vague, unreasoning fear of something—I knew not what. I was on the docks, lying behind some barrels, and was wearing filthy seaman's clothing, and did not have one scrap of identification on me, or one cent of money. I felt hunted, terrified, and my one thought was to escape, so I signed on the first ship leaving Savannah that would take me as an extra hand. I was obviously under age, but a shipmaster who is anxious to complete his crew and get underway will sometimes overlook such a shortcoming, particularly if it suits his convenience to do so. It was an English ship bound for London and all he wanted from me was a name, which I gave him. Jack Ransome. I pulled it out of a hat, or should I say, a keg of Madeira wine that I noticed on the dock being unloaded, labeled RANSOME SHIPPING COM-PANY. The crew asked no questions—there were too many like me on board to bother with one more man, who wished to remain anonymous."

"On that voyage, however, when my head cleared and my senses were restored to working order, I determined to return to Savannah and find out who I was. It is hard now to explain why I didn't," he added musingly.

"Perhaps you would oblige us by trying," Victor said with exquisite sarcasm.

"Yes," Uncle Charles agreed, "I find that incom-prehensible, myself."

"Terror," Colin replied. "Pure, unreasoning terror. Of the unknown. Of the thought of walking blindly into a trap. Of learning something I would not want to know. I was only sixteen, remember, and have always been cursed with an overactive imagination," he added apologetically.

But he hadn't. It was I who had been the imaginative one, and Colin who had been the scoffer, the disbeliever, the one who had said, "You have no need of goblins or ghosties to explain away your fears, Sarah. Face up to them with the truth and you'll find they have a habit of shrinking in the light of reason." Yet, in spite of his, and later, Grandfather's bracing words, I had continued to be sensitive to the atmosphere surrounding people near me. But it could not be from Colin, the pragmatic one, that I was now receiving a palpable impression of steady, unrelenting fear. It had been there for some time, triggered, no doubt, by something Colin had said, but now it was growing stronger and seemed to concern me, to reach for me with icy tentacles. My own fear rose sharply, fed by that other's, and my heart began beating as wildly as the frantic wings of a trapped bird. Colin was talking, and I glanced cautiously about. The others were watching him steadily, but no one's face wore the blinded, whitened look that I was certain must betray my own. Colin continued to be unaware of my predicament, and gradually, with the aid of deep breaths, I managed to relax, to swamp my terror with reason while viewing it objectively. Was it mine, or another's? Already, whatever frightened me was receding, and from a comfortable distance, began to seem like a foolish aberration. I could imagine Colin's scoffing if he knew!

With an effort, I put my mind to what Colin was saying, words that were factual and surely gave no reason to inspire terror. It seemed that during all those years that we suffered, and mourned him, Colin had been leading a full, rich life, having discovered that the slight hankerings after the sea that had stirred him as a boy had grown into a greater yearning now that he was a man. He would have continued his roving indefinitely, he added, had he not found within himself a more compelling instinct—a love for land. The British Government was encouraging emigration to Canada, and he applied for farmland with money he had saved from his voyages. Not surprisingly, he soon realized that he also possessed a talent for knowing the better points of a racehorse. So, for the past year, he had been following the racing circuit, attending sales, and "perhaps, even seeing you there, Victor, since Grandfather tells me that you have been representing Saramount in the past."

In the past. The implication was clear. If Colin had wished to infuriate Victor, and it had begun to seem that he was deliberately inflicting a few jabs for that purpose, he could not have made a better choice of words. But Victor had himself in hand now, and although he was smoldering, he did not explode, as I half expected him to do. His eyes narrowed suddenly to glittering slits, but he said nothing.

"This is all very interesting." Uncle Charles rose and returned his cup to me with a courtly bow. "I myself have heard of this—amnesia, it is called—and I believe that terror is one of its symptoms. However, it is also easily imitated; therefore, you must expect some skepticism on our part. As I am sure you do. But back to your story—apparently, you have begun to recover your memory?"

"Yes." Colin's voice was as smooth as his interrogator's. "Gradually, about a year ago. Only a little at first, like outlines dimly perceived in a fog, then abruptly, a month ago, almost entirely. That is when I came home. I remembered Grandfather, Sarah, everyone—and I knew that I must find out what had happened to them. I wasn't even sure of my reception for, of course, I realized that by now I must be considered as dead. But something happened to me twelve years ago, and I must clear up that nagging mystery. I hoped that familiar surroundings might do it, for until I know what happened and why, I won't feel safe here."

It was a declaration of hostilities. And the terror was back, more restrained, but someone in this room was very frightened. Uncle Charles sat down abruptly, his face a study. It was out in the open now—obviously Colin believed that his attack originated from Saramount. And now I thought of another oddity, one that I was sure Colin had already considered. No less than what happened to him, was the question of why he had left earlier than he was supposed to. I remembered the gypsy fair—vividly, for one so young at the time—but I could remember nothing that would explain the unexplainable: Colin's sudden decision to leave without saying goodbye to me or to Grandfather. His ticket had already been purchased, of course, but why did he decide to use it then? Why did he pick up his valise, slip carefully downstairs without awakening anyone, and walk the three miles to Talley, where he caught the midnight train to Savannah and the destiny that awaited him there? He must have passed the fairgrounds, where so recently there had been merrymaking. It would have been quiet by then, with a few campfires glowing in the dark, etching the outlines of the caravans and the string of tethered horses. Did the dogs bark, I wondered, and did a few, perhaps, follow at Colin's heels, nipping? Did a babe awaken, crying, disturbed by the noise, and was it hushed and soothed by its mother? The gypsies had not said and, if Colin did not remember, no one would ever know now, for the gypsies were a wandering, restless lot, and many thousand miles and thousands of nights had passed since that night.

Perhaps, though, the gypsies—one of them—had robbed Colin and struck him down, then dressed him in the old clothes in which he found himself. He would have had to follow him to Savannah to do so, for the conductor remembered an alert young face under the hair and cap when he punched his ticket. Colin was not injured then.

Grandfather crisply struck down the theory I timidly advanced. "The gypsies were thoroughly investigated at the time. They were found camping at Goose Creek and all their numbers were present. No attempt had been made to flee, as they would have surely done if one of them had committed a crime. No, I think we can dismiss the gypsy involvement, Sarah."

"But not the rest of Sarah's theory," Uncle Charles said thoughtfully. "It is possible that someone followed him onto the train and attacked him later for what money he was carrying. Or for some other reason that is at present incomprehensible," he added reluctantly.

Victor, at that, rapped out a loud, incredulous oath and leaped to his feet so violently that I started and spilled tea all over Uncle Marion's blanket.

"Poppycock," he snapped. "A collection of half-baked theories! Can't any of you see what this impostor is doing? He is involving you in his story, trying to get all of you to speculate on it, solve his mystery for him, because he has no reasonable explanation of his own to advance! If we keep this up, he'll have us all suspicious of one another, wondering what happened, even believing that one among us attempted murder!"

"Why don't you believe him, Victor?" Grandfather asked slowly.

"Instinct. Intuition. Call it what you will, but I know he is not Colin!" Victor ground the words out through his teeth, and the glare he threw at Colin was murderous with hatred. "He is most persuasive, I grant you that. And I cannot put my finger on the falsity in his story, but I swear to you he is an impostor! He has used a chance resemblance to a dead boy to advance his claim to a fortune. He has help, of course," he added quietly. "He couldn't do it without assistance from someone close, probably someone in this room." His eyes roved. "Personally, I plump for dear little Sarah. No one else would have a reason to ring in an impostor, but she has always wanted her beloved Colin home. She has never believed he was dead. This man could have gotten in touch with her, convinced her that he was Colin, then pumped her dry of information."

My face flamed. "That's not true!" I cried outraged.

"My dear boy, now you are positively reaching for straws." Grandfather's voice was a mixture of exasperation and amusement. "If this man is an impostor and is getting assistance, then it cannot be from Sarah, cloistered as she has been within the walls of Millhaven. Better say Madeline, or me, the two people who have your interests most at heart. However, never fear, my son, I am not accepting Colin's story without investigation. I expect soon to hear from our embassies in England and Canada and I am having other inquiries made. I have already told Colin this, and he accepts the necessity. In the meantime, until we establish our facts, I suggest—indeed, insist—that we observe the amenities of courtesy and good breeding."

His steely-gray eyes looked directly into Victor's stormy brown ones until, at last, with a half-snort, half-sob, Victor stood up and strode toward the door.

"Very well, Uncle Abner. If you insist, I will remember that I was bred a gentleman. And I shan't distress the others by repeated doubts of your guest's identity until you receive your proofs. But my mind remains unchanged!"

"I always had to prove myself to you, Victor," Colin drawled lazily. "You were always a hard devil on me. Have you forgotten the time you taunted me into riding that big bay gelding of Grandfather's and I almost broke my neck?

I have often wondered if you were disappointed that I didn't."

Victor looked at him steadily. "Any one of a dozen people could have told you that story," he commented.

"Yes," Colin replied blandly, "and you'll never believe that one of them didn't, will you?"

CHAPTER 3

I went looking for Mammy. Late afternoon, before it was time for her to return to the house and begin the simple preparations for supper, was the best time to find her alone. I found her in a fresh apron on the porch of her cabin, rocking, while she gazed out across the fields at the westering sun. Colin and I had been Mammy's children, and I knew she would understand even better than Grandfather what I was feeling now. I sat on the top step and rested my head against her ample lap, and I did not even have to tell her. She knew.

"Ah 'member how it was wit' you whin you fin' him gawn," she said softly. "Night befo', aftah Ah git to bed, Ah heah whippo'will cry an' Ah knowed bad luck was comin'. Next mawnin', Nathan had already bin upstairs an' foun' his room empty, whin Ah git to th' kitchen. He come down an' tole me, Colin, he gone, his valise, he gone, too. An' he shakin' his head, an' sayin', Doan' unnerstan' why he didn' wait to say goodbye to Sarey. Whut we gwine do wit' thet chile now? Ah knowed Ah'd have trouble whin you come down, an' sure enuff, trouble, he come. Ole Man Trouble, he fly right in th' windo', an' he ain't nevah flyed out agin. You scream an' scream whin Ah tole you, Colin, he alreddy lef', an' you fought an' bit an' scratch, whin Ah try to hole you. You run right through th' house in yo' nightgown, screamin' fo' him, an' yo' gran'pap, he come outta his room an' try to hesh you, an' you keep on a-runnin', right out th' do' an' toward th' woods an' th' swamp. Nath', he want to sen' aftah you; Nath', he skerred you gwine to git snake bit or sink in th' quicksand, but Mistah Abnah, he say, leave her alone, Nate; she knows them woods lak she knows th' back of her han', an' she won't come to no harm. She'll come home whin she figgers out Colin'll be back in a few months, an' it ain't th' end of th' worl'."

"I don't remember that, Mammy," I said dreamily.

"Ah doan' think you 'member much at all 'bout thet time, Sarey," Mammy said. The dark eyes, sunken deep in the wrinkled cheeks, rested on me enigmatically. "You come home jes lak Mistah Abnah say, late thet aftahnoon, 'bout mos' dark-time. You showed up at th' liberry windo', in yo' long nightgown, wit' yo' hair all tangles an' yo' feet muddy an' scratch; an' yo' gran'pap, he jes hole out he arms, an' you jes crept right in them. It was a bad time fo' you, Sarey, th' beginnin' of th' bad times. You ain't nevah bin happy since thin, not really, fo' you was always missin' him."

"But now he is home, Mammy," I protested eagerly. "The bad times are over and we can be happy."

Mammy's toil-worn hand stilled where she was stroking my hair. "So they says," she said dryly.

I twisted around to look at her. "Don't you believe it is Colin, Mammy?" I asked fearfully.

"He a man, now," she said evasively, "an' Ah keeps lookin' fer th' boy. Colin, he was my baby, an' Ah keeps lookin' at th' eyes. It's th' eyes Ah goes by."

I waited and finally asked, "And are they Colin's eyes?"

"Th' eyes, they doan' seem right somehow. But Colin, he call me 'Mammy' in thet funny voice of his, an' hug me, an' I guess it's him."

"He remembers a lot of things about the past, Sister says."

"He sho' is makin' up to Miz Madeline," Mammy said darkly. "Ev'ry night, they walks out. Mistah Victah, he doan' lak it nohow."

I was silent, partly from shock. Colin—and Madeline? But Mammy would know all about them, and the fact that Victor was jealous, both of Madeline and of Colin's new position. She would also know, somehow, that Grandfather was uncertain about Colin, but that his plans for him did not include me, Sarah, the little cousin who had not yet grown up. No, there would be no secrets from Mammy.

And for the first time, there seemed to be no secrets from me, Sarah. Everyone wanted to seek me out for confidences. It was a rare experience for one who had always been the most unimportant member of the family. When Aunt Lucy tapped at my door a short time later, then came in and closed it behind her with all the signs of wishing to have a heart-to-heart talk, I was taken aback. We had always existed on terms of mutual ill will, but whereas mine was merely a strong dislike, hers had seemed tinged with actual malevolence. However, she was exerting herself to be friendly. She wore a big smile that reminded me unpleasantly of a grinning crocodile, and her voice was as sweet as a cloying treacle pudding.

"Sarah, do you think that young man, Colin—if that is indeed his name—is interested in Madeline?"

I stared at her in astonishment, wondering at her choice of priorities. Colin, if that was indeed his name and if his claim held true, could destroy her son's future, but it was unimportant to her, obviously, so long as there was a chance that Victor and Madeline were parting and breaking their long understanding. It had always been uneasily understood that Aunt Lucy's love for her son bordered on obsession, self-centered, all consuming, so that it left no room for anything else but an equally violent hatred of her rival, Madeline. Victor had been able, in the past, to protect Madeline partially from his mother's virulent excesses, but if he withdrew his support, as now seemed possible, the hostility that simmered beneath the surface would break out. I felt a spasm of pity for Madeline, remembering a long-ago occasion when Colin and I had come upon her, shivering, head bowed, while Aunt Lucy raved at her for some minor childish sin. Grandfather and Victor had both been absent, so that it had been up to Colin to tweak the lion's tail, divert her angry attention to him so that Madeline could escape, and he had done so with a defiant bravado that had not masked his own shrinking dread.

"Well?" she demanded impatiently. Her eyes were bright and her cheeks highly flushed.

"I haven't been here long enough," I said carefully. "I would have to have time to—"

"Time!" she snapped. "You've been here long enough to see what I've been seeing this past week! You've seen her new clothes, the change in her! Something is afoot! Every night they walk in the moonlight and Victor sits in a corner and scowls. I should think you'd need no more time than you already have had. When it comes to Colin, I would think you'd have second sight!"

I flushed. Her words rattled me and, before I knew what I was saying, I found myself repeating some of what Madeline had told me, all the while loathing myself for my easy capitulation. ". . . We thought he might be Grandfather's choice for Rose," I stammered to a halt.

She seemed surprised, then thoughtful. "Sarah, I want *you* to marry Victor," she said insistently. She seemed to have no idea of the audacity of her command, nor that the notion might be appalling to me. "He and Madeline are at daggers-drawn right now, and I know my boy. He won't allow her to play fast and loose with him. If you strike now, while the iron is hot, you can get him! I'll help you, by speaking to Abner about making the match."

I blinked at her, visited by a flash of panic that, if she persisted, she might succeed in bending me to her single-minded will. "Aunt Lucy! Stop! You know I am not interested in Victor, and he certainly isn't in me! You mustn't plan on anything like that, or allow him, or Grandfather, to think I will agree to it."

It was as though I had not spoken. "Help me," she went on feverishly. By now, small flecks of foam beaded her lips and her eyes were flickering with dancing lights. "Help me with this, and I will help you. Between us, we can get rid of Madeline! You won't have to be a wife to Victor—I'll take care of all the arrangements myself. Charleston—the gaiety there—think what fun it will be—"

Really frightened by now, I managed to ease her out of my room by uttering soothing promises that I knew would rise to trouble me later. When I had finally closed the door on her contorted face, I put a chair under the knob and went over to my washbasin, where I scrubbed my hands ruthlessly. Just as thoroughly as I used to do, when I was naughty and was sent upstairs by Mammy to scrub the hands that stole the cookies or broke the cup in the pantry. Not that they had been bad this time: they had merely touched something unclean. I was still shuddering with revulsion when I went downstairs for supper.

Supper at Saramount was a simple meal. One served one-self from the dishes on the sideboard, with Nathan standing by to fetch, and tonight one of Shand's little boys hunkered against the wall, dreamily pulling the rope to the overhead fan that stirred the air lazily back and forth above us.

In honor of my first night home, Mammy had stirred up

a pan of hot spoon bread, which, with a pat of her new butter, was a dish worthy of a company dinner. There was a platter of cold meat, some early tomatoes and strawberries from the conservatory, and milk, fresh from the deep well and so cold that the sides of the pitcher were beaded and frosted with droplets of moisture.

Since Victor had promised to shelve his animosity for the time being, by mutual consent, controversial subjects were avoided and the conversation proceeded amicably, but I wondered if anyone else felt the tension that was at times so thick it could have been cut with a knife. The behavior of Aunt Lucy, for instance. Her eyes roamed unceasingly from Madeline to Colin, then to Victor, and she oozed a sparkling malice. And, having been forewarned by her and Mammy, I now saw the signs of a beginning flirtation between Colin and Madeline, and I perceived a new dimension to Victor's hostility.

"Victor, my boy, do quit fretting and resume your seat. You have been restless since suppertime."

Admonished by Grandfather's words, Victor flung himself into a nearby chair and glumly surveyed the polished toes of his black evening slippers. We were drinking our coffee, but he had finished his in one gulp, then proceeded moodily to destroy the drawing-room fire by vicious jabs with the poker. It had needed a fire to offset the chill rising from the bare, polished floor, inadequately covered in its center by a priceless Chinese rug. The room's paneled walls were painted a creamy white, but the cool colors of gilt and ice blue, which were reflected in the upholstered Chippendale furniture and some of the ornaments scattered about, contributed to the frosty atmosphere. Within my memory and the memory of Grandfather, the room had remained unchanged, each chair in precisely the same position, each ornament occupying its own special niche, from the eighteenth-century Meissen figurines beneath Sarah Mountain's portrait to the well-bred little Dresden group entitled "Love's a-Pleading" on the table beside Grandfather's chair. The only warmth of color was provided by Sarah's magnificent portrait, with its glowing skin tones and the rich, russet shades in her hair.

I was the last person to enter the room and pick up my coffee, which I did not really want although it had been poured and left for me on the sidetable. I seated myself beside Uncle Marion, who seemed rather isolated from the others. Noticing him eying the cup in my hand, which I had sugared liberally and cooled with cream, I leaned forward impulsively and carefully placed it between his cupped palms. An engaging little twinkle grew in his eyes as they met mine, and he tremblingly raised the cup to his lips.

I have since asked myself many times if I could have prevented what happened that night and I am told no, that it was already too late for the old, sick man beside me. But I bitterly regret my neglect, which manifested itself in the absent-minded way in which I casually removed his cup, after he had drained it in quick gulps, then promptly forgot him as we were all prone to do. I was, of course, on edge, fearful of a repetition of my frightening experience that afternoon, and also, feeling rather exhausted, the effect, no doubt, of having received too many confidences in too short a time.

Of course, Grandfather riveted our attention immediately with his first words: "Something was said that appealed to me very much this afternoon." He eyed the smoking fire and Victor with equal disapproval. "That was when Colin suggested that he and Sarah might clear up part of his missing memory by discussion. Although Victor did not precisely approve of the idea," he added with a glint of irony,

"I would, nevertheless, like an account of what each of you remembers that night."

This time, Uncle Charles objected. He had been chatting with Madeline, his demitasse lightly balanced on one elegantly clad knee, and he seemed loath to be dragged into a discussion of Colin's problems. "Abner, can anything be gained by this rehashing of an old unpleasantness?" he protested. "And is it possible you are inferring that we need an alibi for that night?"

"Insofar as you can remember, yes, I think an alibi would be very helpful," Grandfather replied coolly. His hooded eyes studied the flush that stained Uncle Charles's cheekbones. "If you remember, you never had a chance to give yours, since you and Rose were already gone by the time Colin was reported missing."

"Very well." The flush had receded, leaving an austere face stripped white of color. "As I remember, we were conveyed to that foolish carnival in the buggy while the children walked. I would have preferred staying at home, but the house was emptying, and Rose was excited. I could not expect anyone else to take on the task of looking after her. As it was, I had my hands full. She got away from me several times." His eyes clouded. "With a girl as lovely as Rose, there is always a boy around. As I remember, she attracted the attention of a gypsy boy." He stopped abruptly. "But this has nothing to do with Colin, whom I don't even remember seeing there at all—or, as a matter of fact, any of you—in the crowd. By the time we returned to Saramount, some of the others had returned too, for bedroom lamps were lit."

"Interesting," murmured Grandfather. "I returned in the buggy, after waiting to see if I would have any passengers, but apparently everyone else chose to walk. Do you remember which bedroom lights?" he added.

"No!" snapped Uncle Charles. "I was tired and went immediately to bed."

"And you left a day or so later and have never returned until now. Why, Charles?" Grandfather asked curiously.

Uncle Charles stirred slightly. His eyes searched the fire, as though seeking the answer there, and when his reply came, I felt it was an evasive one. "Rose was growing up. She needed a home. We had been leading a nomadic life— Saramount, Paris, back to New York, then on to some spa or other. I had no inclination to seek a successor to Louise, but I was determined to find a wife."

"But you didn't?"

"No. It took all my energy to handle Rose—she became involved with a bohemian crowd in Paris—" His voice trailed off dully. Grandfather watched him pityingly, but he did not seem disposed to finish.

"What about you, Madeline?" Colin asked briskly, bringing us back to the present. "What do you remember about that night?"

"The gaiety, the excitement, the dark, sinister gypsies," Madeline said lightly. Her eyes flashed provocatively at Colin. "I was with Victor," she added, demurely, "and we looked at the horses the gypsies wanted to sell. We were together all of the time, weren't we, Victor?"

He cleared his throat. "Yes."

"Not *all* the time." Aunt Lucy had been sitting at her needlework, waiting with all of the quiet tenacity of a spider playing out its line, allowing its victim to entrap itself. Now she was triumphant at having caught Madeline in a lie of her own making. "I went looking for Victor and found him alone. Later, I sent his father to find him, and he came back and told me he was alone."

"We were together," Madeline repeated stubbornly. "I

heard you asking for him and I hid so you wouldn't see me. Behind the wagons."

"Why did you hide?" Colin asked, surprised.

She flushed and cast a shamefaced look at Victor. "It was easier to hide to avoid a scene—"

"I asked her to hide," Victor interrupted crossly. "Father knew, of course—"

"You lie, my son!" Aunt Lucy hissed. "Your father told me the truth—"

As though in defiance, Uncle Marion answered her with a stertorous snort. As was his custom, sometime earlier his head had fallen forward upon his chest in what I assumed was a light doze. Everyone's eyes turned to him as, suddenly, he sagged forward. Only Victor's quickness in leaping up and catching him saved him from toppling out of the chair.

"Father," Victor cried. "What's wrong?"

"Uncle Marion?" I asked, then screamed as Victor tilted the head backward to reveal a blackened, contorted face, the pupils of the eyes distorted to pinpoints, a trickle of spittle trailing from the gaping mouth.

"He's having a fit," shrieked Aunt Lucy, and promptly fainted, thereby forcing Uncle Charles, who might have been of more practical help elsewhere, to deal with her.

Grandfather would not leave his brother's side, although his strength was not equal to helping Victor carry his father to his room. Colin had hurried away to order one of the horses saddled, and a servant sent for the doctor. It was the most helpful thing he could have done, but he returned to a distracted scene of disorder, with Victor attempting in vain to remove his father from it. In the end, however, it made no difference, for although they soon made Uncle Marion comfortable on his bed and brought in cold compresses, and a hot iron for his feet, he was dead by the time the doctor arrived.

The doctor carefully made his explanation. Uncle Marion had been poisoned by the administration of a narcotic drug, as yet undetermined, but probably the sleeping draught which he kept in his room. An enormous amount had been ingested into his system, an amount that would have been dangerous to a healthy person, but was lethal to a man in his condition. His paralyzed muscles, his weakened condition, but more importantly, his doubled-over posture, which had cut off the air passage to his lungs, had induced asphyxia. "If he could have been straightened out in time, or if his vomit had not regurgitated into his lungs —" murmured the doctor, carefully staring at a point above Grandfather's head. "As it was—" He stopped, shrugging fatalistically.

We eyed the doctor questioningly. His attitude was peculiar, diffident—almost embarrassed. Victor, who had come in at the end of his explanation, bluntly made clear what the doctor was hesitant to put into words.

"It was suicide," he said in an expressionless voice. "Dr. Mueller did not want to tell me, but I got it out of him. It *was* his sleeping medicine, and it had been taken recently. There was no possibility of an error, for I sent Madeline back to look around his chair, and she found this." He held up the empty medicine bottle.

Dr. Mueller looked uncomfortable. "Did he have anything to drink within the last half hour?"

"My coffee!" I cried. "I had already sweetened it for myself, but he wanted it, so I gave it to him. I didn't bother to get myself another cup."

"And sugar would hide the taste, so he would not grimace," the doctor said slowly.

"There was no possibility of an accident?" Grandfather asked. He was gray with shock.

"Oh, my dear sir, no possibility whatsoever! I mean—well, what do you think?" the doctor twittered.

"Of course it wasn't an accident," Victor said harshly. "I accept it as suicide, and you must too, Uncle Abner. It was not unexpected. The inquiries, the disgrace, for a man of my father's feeble health, all of this has been unbearable." His eyes moved to Colin. "It is all *your* fault," he added bitterly. "You and that accomplice of yours. You started this nonsense—something like this was bound to happen! What did you expect it to lead to if you came back, asking questions, reviving old wounds! Why did you insist on arousing all this suspicion that had been allowed to rest? Yes, it was all your fault, and I shall never forgive you for it!"

It was almost dawn before I retired to my bedroom. The doctor had found himself with two patients on his hands, for Grandfather, as well as Aunt Lucy, had collapsed. It was left to Victor to see to the arrangements for the funeral as early as possible, but he had fiercely refused Colin's help, and had just as gratefully accepted Uncle Charles's, in preparing his father for burial.

I sat in my window seat, displacing my elderly dolls, and gazed steadily down upon the south lawn while my thoughts jumbled through my brain in hideous disarray. It had been, perhaps, the strangest day in my young life. It had begun with ecstatic happiness at the thought of seeing Colin again, but I knew that would no longer be the thrill it had been last night. His return had been accompanied by too much misery and too many doubts to be the unalloyed delight that I had expected. If he was truly Colin—and even this, apparently, was open to doubt—I knew that I had found him only to lose him again in a different way. In some ways, I thought, it had been more satisfactory as it was before: Colin, caught in a timeless moment of eternity, young, tender, loving only me, and remembered, worshiped even, with all the fervor of a lonely childhood. This Colin was different. He was no longer mine.

I knew that I was concentrating desperately on the subject of Colin in order to avoid having to think about Uncle Marion. I had been suitably grieved while Victor made his careful explanation. Knowing what his life had been, I had even found myself understanding Uncle Marion, who had found the courage to end what had been an intolerable burden. All a sham, a ruse, to numb my emotions and hide, even from myself, the truth. Uncle Marion had not commited suicide. I, alone of them all, knew that there had been no opportunity for an invalid's fumbling fingers to put a narcotic into his cup without my seeing him. Which meant that it had been poisoned before it left the table, by someone who intended murder. I had, until now, successfully beaten down the rising suspicions and sickening questions I must ask myself, but the one that I wriggled and twisted to avoid answering until finally, grudgingly, I admitted its validity was: *whose* murder? Mine or Uncle Marion's? Whose murder was necessary to someone— someone who had released waves of clammy fear this afternoon? I could not be sure that I was the intended victim, for it was not uncommon for me to give my coffee to Uncle Marion. The family had seen me do it a score of times since drinking it was as yet an affectation on my part. Therefore, could I say with certainty that I was the intended victim? My head buzzed and ached with the tension of speculation.

Like a reprieve, I was suddenly arrested by a flicker of movement below me. I leaned forward, pressing against the cool windowpane. A white figure, Madeline's, long skirts fluttering, bound for the summerhouse. Halfway there, she was joined by someone else, a man, stepping out from

where he had been waiting behind a tree. Colin? Or perhaps Victor, her lover? No. After only half a day, I already
knew that figure too well not to recognize it even from this
narrowed view. Somehow that knowledge, or the hard-hit-
ting, improbable events of the day, contributed to send me
weeping to bed, where I finally cried myself to sleep.

CHAPTER 4

Two days had passed since Uncle Marion's funeral, and life, as it must, was returning to normal. I had said nothing of my suspicions—at first, through a superstitious belief that to voice them would somehow make them seem more real; and later, as time went by and I lost my first opportunity to speak, I began to doubt the evidence of my own eyes. Grandfather and Victor, although still grieving, seemed to mourn the tragic waste of his life rather than the fact of his death, and this served to make my confession easier to keep to myself.

Victor, belatedly realizing the effect on his uncle, took care not to reproach Colin again; and as for Madeline and Colin, their intimacy grew. Sometimes, as I watched them, I found myself remembering Victor's wrathful accusation that Colin must have an accomplice, but I could not see why Madeline, loving Victor as she had once done, would bring in someone so harmful to his interests. Then I would tell myself not to indulge in wishful thinking, preferring to see a conspiracy rather than accept the unpalatable truth— Colin was Colin, and this was the beginning of a love affair.

But life went on as before, for April was a month of abundance at Saramount, and everywhere there were signs of that new life. A broody hen strutted about the chicken yard, a cheeping family in her wake, and last night one of the mares had foaled. Victor, who had been up and down all night, had finally taken a pillow and blanket to the tack room and slept there. It had been Bonnie Belle and she had bred true. Paulie brought me the news with my hot water, and when I got downstairs I found Victor and Colin leaving for the stables together, their hostility temporarily forgotten in their shared excitement over the new arrival.

Madeline was sitting alone at the table, hunched over her coffee. The morning sun was dazzling and I noticed how it set her hair aflame, as well as exposing the lines of sleeplessness in her face. The stained tablecloth, littered with orange peels, was unappetizing, and my appetite became peckish as I surveyed the groaning sideboard. This breakfast was no different from any other at Saramount: a mountain of food upon which little impression had been made by earlier diners. There was no diminution in the pyramid of fresh fruit at one end, nor the basket of hot biscuits and cornbread at the other, with oatmeal, thick clotted cream, eggs, sausage, ham, assorted jams and jellies, hominy grits, red-eye gravy and a smoking pot of coffee between.

"Just some coffee, please, Nathan," I murmured, drifting languidly to the table with an orange in my hand.

He was unimpressed. "No, you don't, Sarey," he said sternly. "You cain't do a mornin's work on a cup of coffee. You git yo'self a proper breakfast. If yo' gran'papa knowed you was tryin' to eat lak a bird, he'd be mad, an' you know it."

He watched me with barely concealed amusement as I filled my plate. If he was also directing his words at Madeline, they failed of their purpose, for she didn't look up until I sat down, and then it was to remind me that we were to go to Charleston this morning to see the dressmaker. Custom no longer decreed deep mourning for others of the family than the widow—a black-bordered handkerchief or a neat armband was sufficient; fortunately for me, since the past days had continued to show up the shortcomings of my wardrobe.

Nathan, who was clearing the sideboard, heard her. "No goin' to Charleston today, Miss Madeline. Mistah Abnah ordered th' barouche back in th' stables when he heard about it. I think he wants to see you an' Sarey in th' liberry right aftah breakfast."

"Oh, no," she groaned. "Why?"

"Means he has other plans fo' you, I'd say."

Grandfather was waiting for us with Uncle Charles, and it was hard to tell which man was the angriest. Grandfather's face was highly flushed and his hair stood up in furious white tufts, but it was such a welcome change from his former despondency that I did not mind his temper. A telegram had been delivered, informing him that Rose, who was expected on today's train, had decided instead to arrive on the *Carolina Queen,* which was docking in Charleston harbor at the end of the week.

"It is from a wish to disobey me," Uncle Charles said bitterly. He was white and shaking with rage. "She will do anything to defy me."

Grandfather stopped his tirade to stare at him in astonishment. "I don't see why you think that, Charles. It seems to me that I am the one being defied. You must see how this changes your plans, Sister," he turned to Madeline. "Colin will accompany you to Charleston the day after tomorrow, and you may do what shopping you please. Rose is to be met by eight o'clock the following morning and brought directly here. Sarah, you can wait a few more days for your finery, can't you, child?"

"Of course she can, Grandfather," Madeline said gracefully. "But it is unneccessary for Colin to accompany us. We can manage very well with Shand—"

"Nonsense!" Grandfather snorted. "You two females

can't brave that busy port to look for Rose on your own!
Besides, you will need Colin to see to an extra hack for
her luggage. No, no, my mind's made up."

"I didn't want Colin to go with us," Madeline told me
later, "but I knew there was no moving Grandfather. I
wanted to be in Charleston alone, but instead, he will be
underfoot every minute. Except at night, when I presume
he will be at the hotel and we will be staying with your
Cousin Margaret," she added. "Sarah, I *must* have time for
an errand. If Colin doesn't leave us alone, you must make
some excuse—get him away on some pretext and give me
an opportunity to be by myself for a while."

I agreed, but absently, for my mind was occupied with
an interview I had had with Grandfather after Madeline
and Uncle Charles had left us this morning. He had carefully taken me over the events of the night Uncle Marion
had died, requiring that I tell him exactly how I had
prepared my coffee before turning it over to him.

"But the cup had already been poured and was waiting
on the tray?"

"Yes, Grandfather."

"Strange," he murmured. "I have no recollection of any
of it. We all wandered over to the tray one or two at a time,
after Nathan brought it in and left it on the table." He
caught my eye. "Don't look so upset, honey. I am not
scolding you for allowing your uncle to kill himself. If he
did," he added softly.

How I wished that I had spoken out in the beginning!
But now, to bleat of my doubts would be to bring fresh
unhappiness on Granfather's head. "It could have been an
accident, couldn't it?" I asked hesitantly.

"Too late for that." Grandfather was grim. "The sugar
bowl must be doctored to have it called an accident. There

was, of course, your well-known habit of oversugaring your coffee, but that's chancy. Others use sugar too."

"No," I agreed drearily. "No accident. Because of the sleeping draught under the chair."

"Yes, indeed." Grandfather sounded appreciative. "That was—neat. Once it was obvious that the wrong victim received the overdose, it was easy, in the excitement, to drop the empty bottle near the chair and have it appear to be a suicide. Poor Marion. No one would question his wish to take his own life."

Grandfather's words frightened me, calling up images that I had resolutely throttled back the past few days, but they also broke the gates to my reticence. The words tumbled out, one after another, while he watched me in growing amazement. At the end, still clinging tenaciously to the theory of suicide, I reverted to it.

"Undoubtedly, I was wrong. I looked away from Uncle Marion, long enough for him to put the drug in his cup. After all, Victor said it was suicide."

"He certainly did," Grandfather agreed. "And I have wondered why. There is much about Victor that puzzles me, but this insistence of his that his father had reason to commit suicide—"

"You said 'the wrong victim,'" I interrupted nervously. "Does that mean you think it was supposed to be—me?"

Grandfather did not answer me at once. He leaned forward and packed his pipe with deliberate slowness, then used one flaring, sulphurous match after another in an attempt to light it. As a young man, he had, he once told me, learned to use snuff in the European manner during the Grand Tour he had made before the war. He had brought back a number of jeweled snuffboxes to contain his assortment of exotic brands. When I asked him how it felt to inhale snuff, he had grinned. "Like no other sensation in the world," he had admitted. Later, upon the advice of his doctor, he had taken up the pipe, but he did not crave it, and I noticed he used it most often when he wished to slow a conversation to his own pace. Now he watched me steadily over the flaring matches, as though debating the wisdom of continuing.

"Colin and I talked it over last night," he finally said deliberately. "I have been a weak, sentimental fool, too full of grief to see what was before my nose, until Colin himself pointed it out. He believes that he has endangered your life by suggesting you might be able to remember something that would be dangerous to the person who attacked him."

"Colin said that?" I faltered.

Grandfather shrugged. "Or perhaps he isn't Colin. In this case, it matters very little, since the matter under discussion was your safety. However, if this young man isn't Colin, I cannot understand why he would want you to remember."

"No." I had already thought of that myself.

"And possibly we are all wrong. You did look away, and I am allowing my judgment to be clouded because I do not want to believe that my brother was so unhappy that he took his own life. I am sure that Victor, who seems to be something of a masochist, would interpret my belief that way."

"I can't believe anyone would want to kill me, Grandfather," I protested.

"I hope not," he said soothingly. "I know that if anything happened to you, I would never forgive myself. That is why I am taking the risk of frightening you by this warning. Be careful. Take precautions. The water bottle beside your bed, for instance. Do not drink from it. And watch what you eat and drink elsewhere. Until this cursed mystery of Colin's is solved, you are in danger."

I smiled and bent to kiss him. Surprisingly, my own simi-

lar insecurities had vanished. Like many people who nurse
an unalterable conviction in secret, I was freed merely by
the telling of it. "I promise, Grandfather." But I thought
privately that Victor was right in his assumption. No one
knew better than I that I had no private knowledge that
could harm anyone: I had no secrets to divulge.

Thus it was that I could blame no one but myself for my
folly in not taking Grandfather's warning seriously. Realizing my own ignorance, I assumed that he, Colin's attacker,
would know it too. But I could not be expected to foresee
many things, the first being Madeline's cupidity, as she
strove that night to transfix the interests of not one, but
both of the men present. Not satisfied with just Colin, she
felt a need to continue to tease Victor into a response, in
the teeth of Aunt Lucy's jealous scrutiny. Victor, finishing
a leisurely nightcap with Uncle Charles and Grandfather,
ignored Madeline and Colin, who were conducting an inti-
mate card game in the corner, but I, pretending to be ab-
sorbed in a book, could not help noticing how often her
eyes strayed in his direction.

"It's too early for bed and there's a moon." She shuffled
the cards nervously. "The night's young yet. Remember
how we would go frog-gigging as children, Victor?" She
was overbright, her words tumbling over one another in her
eagerness when she saw him look up casually. "Won't you
please take us?" she coaxed prettily.

He held up his glass to the light as though deliberating. "I
think you and Colin would prefer to be alone," he replied
smoothly, "but I'll certainly take Sarah if she wishes to go.
Would you like to, Sarah?" He seemed blandly unruffled by
Madeline's display of sensibility toward Colin, but I did not
delude myself for one moment, as Aunt Lucy apparently
did when she dropped her head with a satisfied smirk, that
Victor was interested in me, or was reconciled to Colin, to

losing Saramount, or even to losing Madeline. He had merely made a level-headed assessment of the situation in these quiet days since his father's death, and had decided to control his famous temper for the time being while he played a waiting game.

I trailed behind Victor when we went to the stables to look for the spears. He was carrying a lantern but made no attempt to light my way, ignoring my stumbling footsteps and having already forgotten me now that we were alone. Colin and Madeline were some distance ahead: I could see their dancing light by the mill house as we came out onto the lawn.

"We could try here," I suggested, stopping near the edge of the pier.

"Or join the others," he added.

"They don't want us, Victor."

"I know." He had let down his guard, and the desolation in his voice touched me.

He swung the lantern out over the water and I saw the twin gleam of a frog's eyes as I flung my spear. I was never good at this, I thought disgustedly, pulling my spear out of the mud. My aim always went wild at the last moment because I could not bear to impale the frog upon the spear. The lantern swung limply: Victor was gazing absently at his feet.

"Victor," I said abruptly, "if you love Madeline, why did you never marry her?"

He looked up dully, apparently unsurprised that I had correctly read his innermost thoughts. Finally, in a muffled voice, he replied, "There were reasons." He set the lantern down on the rising ground, then took my hand and drew me to sit beside him. "I want to talk, Sarah, and you have always been a sympathetic child. Do you mind?"

"Of course not."

But having begun, he could not seem to continue, although there was no competition for the sound of his voice other than the frogs' comfortable croaking. I waited quietly, momentarily lulled by the hypnotic flow of the smoothly running river, which met no resistance until it reached the old pilings beneath the pier, where it slapped and broke into a widening circle of glitter. The other lantern light had disappeared, or more likely, been extinguished, and ours was the only one sending its homey little glow across the water.

"I know everyone thinks I'm jealous of Colin," Victor said at last, in a husky voice, "but that is not why I am fighting him. I just don't think this man is Colin."

"Do you have a reason for thinking it?"

"No," he admitted. "But what none of you seem to realize is that I *wish* it was Colin! Even though it means losing Saramount, I would give my soul to have him back and all the doubts that have tortured me for years quieted."

"What do you mean?" I faltered.

"That I don't want Saramount at the price of Colin's life," he said grimly. "But I'll be damned if I'll turn it over to an impostor!"

I was silent, shaken. This was not the subject I had expected to discuss with him when we sat down, and try as I might, I could see only one reason for his unequivocal declaration that Colin was an impostor. If he *knew*, beyond a shadow of doubt, that Colin was dead—

"Why can't you accept that you might be wrong?" I asked tentatively. "Are you sure that you aren't believing merely what you want to believe? Why can't you see that his story is plausible?"

He said nothing, but aimlessly stabbed the ground with his spear. His face was sternly outlined as he bent over the lantern.

"You asked why Madeline and I never married. Did no one guess?"

"I presume—because of Aunt Lucy?" I asked hesitantly.

"No. We could have lived with that, but we couldn't live with the question of what happened to Colin."

"Why would that—" I stopped abruptly, fearful that I already knew the answer.

"Matter?" Victor finished it calmly. "The night Colin disappeared, Madeline and I did not return to Saramount together. We knew that Mother would be waiting for us, so we slipped away from the carnival separately. We were only seventeen and eighteen, remember, and we had already experienced years of Mother's rancorous jealousy. As Madeline said, it was easier to run away. So, soon after Father left us, we parted and each went home alone, and I did not see Madeline until dinnertime the next day. All of the talk was of you. Nathan and Mammy were beside themselves with worry, and Uncle Abner not much better off. Rose was upstairs, with one of her interminable headaches, and Uncle Charles obviously concerned with her, poor devil. I remember Father seemed to be in some sort of fog too, and Mother, of course, never has much chatter. There was some speculation about why Colin left early, but not much. No one really questioned it—in fact, it was generally assumed he did it to avoid a scene with you. You were a possessive little beggar," he added dryly. "Then word came from Savannah that Colin was missing, and Uncle Abner left immediately to confer with the police. It was then that Mother came to me and told me that Madeline and my father had been missing that night, and when she taxed him with it, he admitted to getting rid of Colin with Madeline's help. I went mad for a little while, but she assured me that my father, at least, had been acting out of love for me, although Madeline was spurred by an ambition to be mistress of Saramount. I knew, of course, that this wasn't true. Madeline has never been ambitious for herself, but I had to admit that I might have given the impression to her—and Father—that I would overlook anything, even murder, to get Saramount," he added bitterly.

He was looking over my shoulder and I turned to follow the direction of his eyes. Saramount. The moon had briefly disappeared behind the clouds, leaving the house a dark, shapeless mass, but I knew that Victor's eyes, like mine, did not need the moonlight to show him its frail, serene beauty, overlooking the smoothly flowing river that ran past with scarce a ripple, a murmur, on its blindly seeking quest to the sea. If I loved each hand-hewn peg that held this old house together, how much more must this man, who lived within the near-grasp of its ownership? Saramount—a jealous, demanding mistress. Had the price she asked of him been, finally, too much?

"I wanted to get the police at once," he was continuing —and now I could not see his face, only hear the pain in his voice. "But I didn't. He was my father, and it was too late to change anything. He overheard us, Mother and me, talking, and when he came into the room I began cursing him wildly for having saddled me with such a guilt. Mother flung herself between us, babbling nonsense, and Father, instead of answering my charges, made his own, concerning my treatment of Madeline, which had nothing to do with Colin. Finally, he struck me and I knocked him down. You never knew why he had that stroke, did you? Well, among my other accomplishments, the blame for *that* can be laid squarely at my feet! When Father came to, one side of his face was sagging and he was what he remained thereafter. I lived then with the knowledge that I did that to my father, and repeatedly begged his forgiveness, both for the blow and my—obsession. For loving Saramount too much. He gave it, but I don't think I can ever forgive myself."

"Victor, please don't lash yourself so." I put my arms protectively about his bowed shoulders. "What did Madeline say happened to Colin?"

"You don't think I ever asked her about it, do you?" He roused himself to stare at me in a puzzled fashion. "After what I did to my father, after losing this damnable temper of mine, I did not dare! I hoped she would tell me in her own good time, but I could not bring myself to mention it first. How could I marry her, though, knowing that she cooperated with my father in that? Not that I really believe she was aware of what she was doing," he added, defensively.

"But—"

"I have realized since then," he went on, "that I should not have the temerity to resent it if she finds that she can be happy with someone else. Particularly since I took myself out of the running years ago." He laughed shortly. "But you can understand now, can't you, Sarah, that I hold my breath each time that man speaks of trying to regain his memory by picking the brains of the rest of us?"

"Then you aren't sure of him, after all?" I asked triumphantly.

He stood up abruptly and pulled me to my feet. "Not at all," he replied crisply. "I haven't changed my opinion in the slightest. But pushed, with their backs to the wall, who knows what Madeline, or even Mother, might say? To a stranger? And once the law is brought in—"

But Victor was looking better in spite of his confession, or perhaps because of it, and I saw that in allowing his conflict to spill over on me, he had lost some of the bitterness that kept it alive. He was eying me in a slightly bemused fashion, as though wondering at himself in so freely making his confession to me, and when he suggested going in, it was in a brusque way that told me that all confidences were over for tonight. I replied just as abruptly that I wished to remain alone for a while, and asked him to leave me with the lantern.

I wanted to think. I now understood much of what had been a mystery: Victor's hesitancy to commit himself to marriage; Aunt Lucy's purpose in bringing Uncle Marion downstairs, she had used his presence to blackmail Victor into silence, lest he should be rushed in impetuous speech and so betray his father, and Victor's reluctance to have Colin probe the missing hours. But most of all, Victor's certainty that his father had committed suicide, because of the scandal he saw looming ahead when he was exposed. How much of the anger he had heaped on Colin had been directed at himself?

In view of the latter, Grandfather's notion that an attempt was made on my life was nonsense, I concluded complacently. Victor had been right and we had been wrong, after all. But Victor must see that he was no longer able to keep his secret to himself. So long as Colin remained missing, sleeping dogs might lie. But now he surely understood that Grandfather must be told. Perhaps he did understand and that had been his purpose in telling me first. As a bridge to Grandfather. There would be no public repercussions on Uncle Marion's memory of course, for he was dead now, and whether he had actually struck down Colin or had it done, Colin would not wish to pursue the investigation further. As for Madeline, and whatever part she had played, she could not be blamed now. Of course, Colin would be apt to view her with revulsion. With a shrewd flash of intuition, I wondered if Victor was not counting on just that.

I was strolling toward the summerhouse, which was

uphill from the river. I had not needed the lantern after all for the moon was back, brighter than ever. I told myself that my feet were wandering this way by accident, but I knew that I was remembering Colin's and Madeline's assignation. Suddenly, a startled squawk from a wild turkey hen, betrayed by my presence too close to her nest, made me jump.

I had never liked the summerhouse and avoided it when possible. It had been built as a conceit of Colin's mother, back in the eighties, when such things were fashionable. She had imagined herself serving tea outside in a cool, shaded grove, but the surrounding trees cut off the flow of air, the mosquitoes abounded during the hot summer months, and it was too damp and cool to be enjoyed in the winter. Grandfather, through a dislike of seeing anything fall into neglect at Saramount, had kept it and the benches under its roof in good repair, and even had a wooden floor put down for dancing at my sixteenth birthday party. But I had an aversion to the place, an irrational dislike that had nothing to do with its damp location, and now I was dismayed to realize that I was shaking with a chill that was more dread than cold.

I turned in a panic to retreat when a quick rustle behind me alerted me. A woods animal, I thought, turning to look back, and that movement of my head must have saved my life. One of the gigging spears flew past my cheek, its only warning approach a whispering displacement of air, and buried itself in the soft trunk of a pine tree directly in my path. I was stricken immobile for a moment or two, then, with a yelp of fright, I started running, stumbling and partly falling as my feet tangled in my long skirts. I was almost at the house in my headlong flight when I came up against an iron-hard chest and a strong pair of arms, which clasped themselves around me. Colin.

"Here, here, little one! There are no ghosts abroad at Saramount tonight."

"Someone just tried to kill me," I gasped. "With a gigging spear."

He was instantly alert. "Where? Show me."

I hung back. "No, I don't want to go back there."

He kept a firm grip on my arm. "You'll be with me," he said impatiently. "Come on! Show me!"

I trailed back reluctantly to the summerhouse. On the way, Colin stopped for my lantern, and when we came to the stabbed tree he held it aloft while he examined the deep laceration in the trunk. If I had needed any evidence that the spearing was deliberate, I had it, for there was no sign of the spear, although Colin searched the ground under the trees to see if it had fallen.

"So I was right all along! Someone *does* want to kill you!" he exulted in a way that I found totally inappropriate for the occasion.

For the first time, I noticed that he was breathing hard. "You've been running," I said in an accusing voice.

"Of course," he agreed. "I saw your lantern as I started to go inside, and I ran back for you. Little fool, what are you doing out here alone, anyway? Where is Victor?" he snapped. "Come on, let's get away from here." He took my arm and whirled me away at top speed.

"What's the hurry?" I panted as we slowed down.

"I just realized we were bigger fools to return there. He could have still been waiting around to have another go at us with that spear."

"It was your idea to go back, not mine," I said indignantly.

"I know, little one." He was smiling now. "I had to be convinced that you weren't imagining the whole thing. It occurred to me yesterday that the poisoned coffee might have been meant for you, and I asked Grandfather about it. He agreed with me, and was to speak to you about it. Did he not?"

"Yes," I admitted.

"And you were still wandering around alone, at this hour of the night?" he asked sternly. "You need a keeper, if you intend to take such chances with your life! All along, I have been halfway expecting an attack on me, but it had not occurred to me that you might be in danger. However, I think this has proven it. The coffee was poisoned—by someone other than poor Uncle Marion—and it was intended for you. Unfortunately, I have no clear recollection of the episode. We were all milling around the coffee tray, so anyone could have done it. It was chancy—but effective, for you were the last one into the room, and would naturally take the cup that had already been prepared. And confess it—if you hadn't sat down beside your uncle, you would have drunk that coffee! And, feeling yourself growing sleepy, you would have retired at once, with no one to look in on you until the following morning, when it would have been too late."

I shivered. "But it makes no sense," I objected. "I am no threat to anyone—I know nothing at all! And I learned something tonight that solves the old mystery about you, once and for all."

"Oh?" he cocked a questioning eyebrow. "Tell me."

"Not until I've spoken to Grandfather," I said firmly. "And I would prefer you to not alarm him about this—this accident tonight, for I am convinced that is all it is. Someone was gigging—one of the servants, perhaps—and was frightened when he saw what he had almost done."

"And that, too, makes no sense," Colin replied scornfully. "And I certainly shall tell Grandfather about this. At any rate, you and I must talk. How about an early-morning ride—say, seven?"

"Seven!"

He grinned. "All my girls like to get up early to ride with me. Ask Madeline," he added provocatively. "Is seven too late? Shall we say five or—"

"We shall say nine," I said coldly. Madeline, indeed! "I'll see you at breakfast."

But back in my bedroom, I began to shake. Despite my brave words to Colin, I knew that the spearing had been an attempt on my life, and it must follow that it was the second such attempt. True, this had occurred in a shadowed area near the summerhouse, but I had been plainly visible while crossing the lawn, and there was no possibility of an accident, for who would have been frog-gigging more than a hundred feet from the river? Colin had been right to scorn my excuses.

But why? Who would want to kill me now, particularly in view of Victor's confession? Unless it was Madeline, overhearing him, and wishing to silence me.

And that too was ridiculous, I told myself firmly. I was tilting at windmills and needed to talk to someone with a clearer head than mine. Preferably Grandfather, even if I had to awaken him to do so.

I was tiptoeing past Madeline's door when I heard the voices. They were indistinguishable, but undoubtedly a man's and a woman's, hers pleading and his making a stern answer. Madeline, of course, and Victor, giving her an ultimatum? Or Colin, accusing her of a murder? I stood hesitating, tempted to eavesdrop, until I remembered Miss Warren's admonition against such misconduct. It was seldom satisfactory, and less so in this case. My imagination had always been powerful, but I was overreaching this time. Why put such a sinister interpretation on what was no more, probably, than a bedroom seduction scene? I had no need to see Grandfather in my present unsettled mood, so I returned to bed.

CHAPTER 5

I had expected sorrow from Grandfather when I repeated what Victor had told me, but not this grim silence or the burst of furious rage at the end.

"That woman!" he choked. "How could she ruin his life like that, subjecting him to years of torture? She is inhuman!"

"Madeline?" I asked uncertainly.

"Madeline too," he agreed, pacing the library floor. "Both of them forced into immorality because of her!" Seeing my shocked face, he made a visible effort to calm himself. "Don't look so distressed, my dear. In spite of my indignation, I don't intend to murder Lucy, as you may well think."

"Aunt Lucy?" I asked blankly. "You think she *lied?*"

"Of course, she lied," he replied impatiently. "Anyone could see that—knowing her and knowing what sort of man my brother Marion was. And this farce is Victor's guilty secret! Her story wouldn't hold water five seconds with anyone who bothered to check his facts. She was indeed lucky that Marion had a stroke, and I wonder if the poor devil had any notion all those years what his son meant when he asked for forgiveness, or if he believed him merely to be wallowing under the guilt of having knocked him down! Naturally," he added fairly, "Victor would not believe his mother would lie about such a thing, or suspect her of such vindictive cruelty, but I should have thought the fool would have said something to Madeline to give her an inkling of what he thought." But was there a trace of uneasiness mixed with the moral anger overflowing from Grandfather? I was sure of it when he added, "But I'll take care of Lucy—her days are numbered here. In the meantime, I want you to wait before saying anything to Victor. Things must come to a head soon; then all lies will be revealed and the truth told."

"If Uncle Marion is not guilty, then someone else is?" I asked slowly, unwilling to relinquish the security I had felt to know that one mystery, at least, was solved.

"And we're back where we started," Grandfather agreed ironically. "With your life still endangered. Colin told me that there was another attempt last night," he added abruptly.

"Yes," I said miserably. Under the circumstances, I could no longer prattle of accidents.

"There is only one thing to do, my darling. You must talk to Colin at once, tell him everything. As soon as this person learns that you have told all you know," Grandfather said grimly, "then perhaps, you will no longer be a threat."

"But I don't know anything, Grandfather!"

He tooked at me appraisingly. "So you have always maintained," he said coolly. "But perhaps Colin will help you remember."

Colin was waiting for me outside the library door. He was already dressed for riding and was pacing restlessly, beating his crop against his booted legs. He gave me one quick, searching look then. "And did you unburden yourself, Sarah?"

"That's *my* secret," I replied loftily.

He shrugged. "I'll give you five minutes to change," he commented.

My riding habit, an old bottle-green one of velvet, had been cut down for me from one of Madeline's, but with a matching hat trimmed with a curly feather, it did as much for me as it had ever done for her. Colin, I saw from beneath demure lashes, took a second, closer look as I trailed downstairs in less than the five minutes he had demanded.

We went directly to the stables where Traveler and Nellie were waiting, already saddled. Nellie was a nice little mare, gray with four white stockings and a mettlesome, slightly frisky disposition. Traveler was another proposition. Like all racing stallions, he was overbred, nervous, even vicious when unrestrained, and I was surprised that Colin, in his as yet unacknowledged position, was allowed to ride him. The horse was the pride of Saramount and, in the wrong hands, could be ruined. Victor was nowhere in sight, but I knew there must have been an earlier confrontation with him on the subject, and that Grandfather had been adamant that the horse was to be turned over to Colin. Even so, Victor would not have allowed it if Colin had not shown himself to be a superb horseman. Which he was. Holding Traveler's reins in an iron grip, he paced him until we were clear of the house and the outbuildings, whereupon he turned to me with a mischievous grin and said, "Let's let them have their heads, shall we?"

If it had been Bob, my usual, sluggish old mount, I couldn't have kept up. But Nellie was in a heel-kicking mood and Traveler was generous, holding back just enough to give us a feeling of participation in a race, as we flew down the road to the tune of drumming hoofbeats. Colin knew all the old paths and had evidently been taught new ones by Madeline, and we didn't slow down until we were on a road that was gradually dwindling into a lane, and which I recognized as bringing us to the back of the church.

Colin pulled to a halt. His eyes were shining with excitement as he leaned forward and patted Traveler's neck affectionately.

"Aren't we near the church?" he called. When I nodded, he added, "Let's go there. I want to see it."

I was struggling with a confused sense of ambivalence. Now I understood Victor's bewilderment when he insisted that this man could not be Colin, although he had nothing but instinct to back his words. The young Colin had not been particularly interested in horses, one reason Victor had resented his position as future master of Saramount. Could he have changed, made a complete turnaround, as he became older? It did not seem possible, but as I watched, ahead of me, the slim, taut body, the crisp, unruly, red Mountain curls crowning the proud head—truly, so well remembered! I felt my uncertainty dissipate as sureness grew. A person *could* change, I argued: a boy could lose his interest in books and the quieter sports if he was exposed to a continuous life out-of-doors. And for Abner Mountain's grandson, a return to the pursuits of his fathers—land, horses, hunting—would be a natural instinct.

The lane had narrowed now: the trailing moss brushed our shoulders as we passed beneath the trees. Traveler led the way, with Nellie stepping daintily in his tracks. Presently, Colin pulled to a stop and slid off lithely. "Thirsty, Sarah?"

So he remembered the spring. Located behind the churchyard, in a grove of trees just ahead of us, the spring had been used by the congregation since they wrested the land away from the Indians and, in an enthusiastic day of barnstorming, put up the little church. The spring bubbled out of the ground, clear and sweet, and when one bent over to drink, one's reflection was mirrored in the dappled water. A few polliwogs swam about, but they could be scattered with a flick of the finger. The floor of the spring was clear, sparkling sand, and the lip was shored up with bleached white pebbles and shells. It was kept clean by the members when they met yearly to clear the grounds and whitewash the church.

Colin was parting the foliage, leading Traveler by the reins. I slid off Nellie and followed. He tied both horses loosely to a bush so they could crop the long grass and I saw that he remembered where the gourd was kept, hanging on the limb of a tree.

He scooped up some water and handed me a drink and, when I finished, drank after me. His brown eyes danced impishly at me over the top of the gourd, and I knew that he understood my confusion.

"Do you remember a pet name I used to have for you?" I queried idly, prompted by a half-forgotten memory.

"Do you mean 'Rusty'?" he asked casually, rehanging the gourd.

I was shaken. "You *are* Colin!" I cried. "That proves it. No one, not even Victor or Sister, could have told you that! I took the name from a story in a book about a red squirrel that Grandfather read to me, and I used it only in private."

He smiled gently. "If it convinces you, Sarah, then I am glad. But I would not advise you to attempt to convince the others. It would merely strengthen Victor's suspicion that we are conspirators, and do nothing to change his mind."

Yes. Weighed against his own instincts, my small scrap of evidence would be dismissed by Victor as no evidence at all, or merely the proof of conspiracy.

Colin took my hand and led me around the church toward the front.

"Sarah," he began in a manner as though he was speaking to a child. "I believe that two attempts have been made on your life to prevent you from trying to speak of the past. All the more reason for you to, now, so that I can tell the others. If you cannot remember," he added grimly, "then you must be very, very careful."

I looked at him doubtfully. We were at the front steps now and Colin drew me down to sit beside him. The sun was warm as it touched our faces, and the tabby wall felt pleasantly cool to our backs. Colin leaned back on his elbows and stretched out his long legs.

"Now," he began, squinting at me lazily, "we walked along that road there, in front. On our way home. Did anything happen?"

I looked obediently at the road, but nothing stirred in my brain, no teasing memory intruded itself. It remained an ordinary road, dappled with shadows and sunlight, with butterflies dancing above it. I sat up suddenly. Two moon faces regarded me solemnly from the protection of the trees. As I watched, two black and white cows emerged and slumped awkwardly across the road, where they began to munch the grass beside the fence, their bells tinkling an erratic tune as they moved their heads.

"Victor came home with word that he had seen the gypsies pitching camp," I murmured drowsily, watching the cows. "We were excited about it."

"The fair *was* a big event to us, wasn't it?" he agreed.

"Yes. You were kind to me, Colin. I have realized, after growing up a little, how kind. When I grew sleepy that night, you weren't cross, but offered to take me home so that Grandfather could stay and watch the horse auction. You were that sort of boy."

He looked at me oddly. "Thank you, Sarah," he said gently. "And after that, what?"

"We walked home along this road. You had bought popcorn for the next day, and you carried it in your pocket.

Halfway home, I stopped and pulled off my shoes, and you put them in your pocket also. It was a warm September night, remember? When we got home, you took me to my room and put me to bed. I said my prayers to you. I didn't want you to leave," I added with a smile. "I delayed you as much as possible, begging you to stay, to have a picnic with the popcorn. You laughed and said it was too late." I stopped, a puzzled frown on my face. "You were pale," I added uncertainly, "and you looked sick. I asked you if you were sick." I stopped again, for I was feeling sick myself, fluttery and nervously uneasy. I coughed and ran my hands down the sides of my skirt, leaving wet streaks on the green velvet.

Colin glanced at me sharply and took one of my hands in his. "Your face is white, Sarah, and your hand is cold. What's the matter? Do you remember something? Why was I sick?"

"I don't know," I said fretfully. "Please don't ask me any more. You wouldn't tell me, but I think it was the popcorn. You ate too much popcorn, I think."

"But we didn't eat the popcorn," Colin explained patiently. "You said I told you it was too late for a picnic."

"I know." My eyes met his pleadingly. "Please, Colin, don't ask me any more. I don't remember anything more. You left soon afterward, anyway. You stood in the doorway and said, "Goodnight, little sister," and went away. That was the last time I saw you, because I fell asleep and the next morning you were gone."

Colin looked as though he would like to ask more, but instead he nodded and said comfortably, "Very well. We'll talk about it another day. Meantime, why did I leave without saying goodbye, Sarah? Do you have any theories?"

"Some people would say you did it to avoid a scene with me," I muttered, shamefacedly dropping my head.

"But I don't believe that. Do you, Sarah? I wouldn't have hurt you like that, would I?" he countered.

"No, you wouldn't," I agreed and knew with a sudden conviction that it was true. The reassurance that had been shattered by Victor's thoughtless words returned. No, Colin would not have been cruel. He must have had another, overwhelming reason to leave so abruptly, board the train and present a seemingly untroubled face to the conductor.

"Let's drop it, Sarah." Colin rose abruptly and began to slash at the grass with his crop, as though slashing at the answers that continued to elude him. "Let it come naturally. You'll remember quicker that way. Instead, we'll look over the churchyard." He took my hand. "I want you to show me the first Sarah's grave."

I led him to the older part of the churchyard, where beneath the spreading limbs of giant oak trees we read a dim inscription on the moss-covered stone slab.

"Sarah, relict of Abner Mountain—"

He wandered away. "So many of our ancestors married cousins," he remarked idly. "Have you noticed? I guess that is why the red hair continues to crop up, generation after generation."

"Sarah," he called insistently from where he stood before two graves with a common headstone. "Here's something curious. These two people died on the same day, the day I left Talley. September 17, 1898."

"The Harrisons," I said, joining him. "Joe Bob's parents. I guess you would not have heard about them, for Grandfather did not learn of it himself until that night, at the carnival. They drowned in a ferryboat accident near Hatteras about dawn, Saturday morning, and as soon as their bodies were recovered, were sent home for burial. Joe Bob went to pieces. It was after that that he became a drunkard, and gambled away his home." I glanced toward the church. "He is usually to be found around here in the mornings."

To my horror, I saw that my words were prophetic: a pale face, wearing a weak, foolish grin, was peering at us from a corner of the church. Apparently he had been inside, asleep, and was awakened by the sound of our voices. When he saw me look at him, he lurched forward, arms outstretched.

"Ish Colin, ish't? Colin, ole fella, wanna talk."

"I can't involve you in this." Colin gripped my arms and pulled me away. "Come on!"

We ran toward the horses. Colin flung me up into the saddle before untying the reins.

"Colin, ole man! Don' run 'way," Joe Bob quavered. "Ish im-import'n I talk t'you. Come back!"

Colin leaped on Traveler's back and touched his flanks with his crop. We were off in a spurt of dust, Joe Bob's wail of disappointment following us.

"He's harmless," I said apologetically, sorry that on my account Colin had spurned his old friend.

"Yes, I know," Colin agreed, but he didn't turn back. We didn't speak on our return to Saramount, which was conducted at a more moderate pace. On the way, a niggling little doubt tormented me—why had Colin forgotten the location of Sarah Mountain's grave? He had known it when, as children, we had visited the churchyard with wildflowers for his parents' graves nearby.

And if that meant he was not the real Colin, why this insistence that I remember the events of that night he left? Unwillingly, I recalled the uncomfortable experience I had my first day home, the sensation that someone was afraid. Of me. Could it have been Colin? Surely, then, he would prefer me to forget. Unless he wanted to satisfy himself that he had nothing to fear from me. If so, I hoped I had set his mind at rest.

Seesaw, Marjorie Daw, was this the way it would always be, I wondered plaintively—positive one hour, doubting the next? Was I never to be sure? Yet, why would he forget something so important while remembering an obscure pet name I used when we were children?

CHAPTER 6

When Grandfather was a boy, the river was the only
method of getting to Charleston. The roads were barely
passable, sometimes no more than rough tracks leading
from one plantation to another, and traffic was confined almost entirely to the water routes. In fact, his father kept his
carriages at the townhouse in Charleston for the family's
use there, while they summered out the malaria season
away from the swampy night miasmas, which were particularly virulent from May until the November frosts blackened the sweet potato vine.

Grandfather used to entertain me with stories about the
parties at Saramount in those days, when the empty echoing ballroom was thrown open and music from the orches-
tra could be heard for miles across the water. The river in
front of the house would be brilliant with floating lan-
terns, their lights bobbing and twinkling like low-flying
fireflies, and the boats would pull up to the dock to allow
the passengers to disembark, the ladies in their silk and velvet hoopskirts and the gentlemen in superfine creaseless
pantaloons.

The river route was no longer acceptable now for ladies
dressed as Madeline and I were, in our pretty summer
frocks. One followed the King's Highway now to Mount
Pleasant, and from there, was ferried across the Cooper
River to Charleston. It was a pleasant drive at any time,
and that morning the air tingled with the tart coolness of

wine, so that we could enjoy wearing our shawls in the open barouche. The road was shaded with overhanging oaks and trailing moss, and when we reached slightly higher ground we were within sight of the water. Colin sat opposite us, dressed in white linen, while Shand, on the driver's perch, silently guided the team, his reticence a sure sign that he continued to disapprove of Colin. They both wore black armbands.

We had the road to ourselves until we neared Mount Pleasant, where farm traffic made the going slow. The terminal was at the foot of Hibben Street, and we joined a crowd awaiting the next ferry, behind a drummer on a big cob, his carpetbag looped to his saddle.

The ferryboat gave a warning toot as it lowered its plank and the traffic moved forward. It was the *Sappho*, and it boasted, among other luxurious appointments, a curving staircase with brass rails and, imported from Savannah, an Italian string band which played tunes for us as we moved across the water. The carriage fare was expensive, and I appreciated Grandfather's motive in sending Colin along, both as protector and banker.

"Shall I accompany you ladies to the dressmaker?" he asked genially.

Mindful of Madeline's strictures to keep Colin away, I replied quickly, "No, if you please, Colin! Dressmaking is ladies' business."

"Is Charleston so provincial, then?" he teased.

"Charleston is not New York or London," Madeline said sharply, "and we would prefer that you take our valises to Cousin Margaret's and await us there."

"But *I* would not!" Colin answered promptly. "I refuse to be fed to the old dragon without you two at my back to protect me. No, I'll amuse myself in my own way and meet you there later."

Standing at the ferry rail, I watched Charleston draw near, a huddle of narrow two- and three-story buildings with three church spires breaking the skyline. The ferry docked at the foot of Gaillard Street, which led by way of cobblestoned streets to the heart of a city that had, for the most part, remained unchanged since the day that Abner Mountain arrived by sailing ship with his bride. Had he and Sarah, perhaps, passed this same stately white house with its blank, aloof shoulder presented to the street, while hiding its garden behind the high, brick wall? Had they caught a tantalizing glimpse through an iron grille gate, and had the lush, tropical growth seemed alien to cool English eyes? I thought so, for Sarah had planted primroses at Saramount—they were there even to this day.

We were bound for King Street and the small, thriving shops there. Much care had to be exercised by Shand in guiding the team through the streets, for they were narrow and choked with traffic. I heard him muttering imprecations down upon the head of a driver of a sober-sided black buggy, whose wheels had barely missed scraping ours.

Mrs. Hillman, the dressmaker, had made progress. Several dresses were ready for me. The tucks and pleats and braids of Miss Warren's day were out, along with the bustle and the whaleboned corset. Natural waistlines, flowing skirts, loose sleeves and wide berthas were the rage, and my petite reflection reassured me that the rich, creamy lace and soft fabrics molding my bust and hips eradicated forever the impression of childishness.

Madeline fidgeted throughout the fittings and while arrangements were made for delivery of the remaining garments to Cousin Margaret's house. We were outside, each carrying a bulky hatbox, when I learned, with a resigned lack of surprise, that she had in mind a destination other than the trim little house on Tradd Street. However, we were seated at a table in the St. John Hotel, our dinner ordered, before I learned her real purpose.

"You have probably guessed that it concerns Colin," she informed me. "He let slip something that made me suspicious of him. As you know, his story is that he recovered his memory a month ago. He lied. He was in Charleston as far back as Christmas."

"How do you know?" I took a careful sip of water.

"He apparently attended the Christmas communion services at St. Michael's. As you know, the bishop was so exhausted at the end, he had to be assisted from the altar. Colin commented on it casually," she explained eagerly, "saying that he was sorry to see the old gentleman so feeble. He was vexed when he noticed the slip and tried to gloss over it and I pretended not to notice." She beckoned to a waiter. "Will you ask Mr. Callahan to join us for coffee?"

He looked surprised. "Yes, ma'am."

"Stop looking so shocked, Sarah," she hissed. "If I am willing to strike up an acquaintance with that horrid little creature at the front desk, then you should be willing to remain here and play gooseberry! Surely you are as anxious as I am to learn the truth about Colin!"

But I wasn't. I made that unhappy discovery as I watched the smirkingly obsequious desk clerk bowing over Madeline's hand, flattered to be sought out by a Mountain of Saramount, and fawningly eager to do anything—yes, anything!—to oblige such a prominent person as Abner Mountain. I gazed fixedly at my plate and tried not to listen as Madeline spun out her story for him. And all the while, I knew that I did not want Colin to turn out to be an impostor.

Grandfather had warned me to beware of falling in love with Colin, but even then it had been too late; and to my surprise, the discovery that Madeline was not, was the least important of the emotions that beset me.

The desk clerk was an ambitious man, albeit an uneasy one, for he knew he had no authority to turn his registry book over to Madeline. However, he could not hold out before her inflexible purpose, so it wasn't long until we were seated behind the desk, the book spread out before us. She quickly found what she was seeking. The signature, Jack Ransome, registered for the dates of December twentieth through January eighth. Three weeks! Four months before Colin had gotten in touch with Grandfather, he had been in Charleston and had spent three weeks here—doing what? Familiarizing himself with the surroundings? Learning all he could about Saramount? Preparing himself for the questions he would be asked later? Conferring with someone— his partner in crime, perhaps?

Madeline was elated. With effortless ease, she made the natural jump from Colin the heir, to Colin the impostor. With the discovery in the registry, and in spite of my reminding her that it proved nothing, she was already positive that she could unmask him. If I had not been so miserable, I would have been amused by the haughtiness with which she dismissed Mr. Callahan, now that he had served his useful purpose, and swept out into the lobby, to come face to face with Colin.

He made a quick assessment of the situation. "If I didn't suspect that she gulled you like a fish on a line," he said gently to the gaping clerk, "I'd have your job for this." He made a sweeping bow to us and crooked both elbows. "Ladies? Shall I escort you to the carriage? No, don't speak, Madeline," he continued, after we were outside, "I know what you are going to say. I remember the slip I made about the bishop, and if I didn't, the looks of guilt on

Sarah's face and defiance on yours would tell me what I wished to know."

Madeline jerked free. "And what do you intend to do about it?" she demanded. "You can't stop me from going to Grandfather the instant I get home and telling him just what I found!"

"Do," he replied cordially. "I expect you to do just that. Of course, you won't tell him a thing he doesn't already know, but he will be glad to learn how busy you have been on his behalf."

The expression on Madeline's face was ludicrous. "Grandfather knows?"

"Of course. Before we left Charleston, I told him everything. After all, Madeline, you haven't unearthed a crime. I have merely failed to give you every detail of my life up to returning to Saramount. If that indicates guilt, then you're entitled to your spot of detective work!" His accent had never been so strong. In spite of his ironical reproof, I saw that he was thrown off balance.

Madeline's face was a study as we approached the barouche waiting quietly for us at the corner of Broad Street. Colin was looking extremely virtuous as he handed us into it, and I wondered if he would disarm Cousin Margaret as easily as he had bested Madeline.

I was right: Cousin Margaret was charmed with Colin. She sat on her piazza that afternoon and rocked and waved her fan gently, while he charmed her right out of an invitation to remain at her house. He had delivered us and our valises, then made a half-hearted attempt to return to the hotel where he was to obtain a room. But Cousin Margaret delayed him to "sit a spell," which he did while telling her stories of his sea voyages, of England and Barbados and other places she had visited when she was young.

"I declare, I haven't been so well-entertained in yeahs!" She patted gently at her damp little roly-poly face, red and beaming with delight. And somehow, when Colin mentioned again that he must leave, she discovered that there was a room upstairs available for her "gentleman caller"; word was sent to Shand to stable the horses and it was settled.

"It's just potluck tonight," she added. "A shrimp pilau and a sweet, but I'll tell my cook to spread herself a little, since we have such a chawmin' guest!"

"And how easily he worked it," Madeline told me darkly when we were alone in our room. She was heating her curling iron down the lamp chimney, and her pretty face twisted into a grimace as she tested it with a wet forefinger. "Now he won't have to worry about us, or what we might discover, since he's in the same house to keep an eye on things!"

That night, Colin escorted the three of us to the Hibernian Hall, where we attended a musicale performed by local artists. The ordeal was prolonged by the serving of weak sherry and dry little seedcakes afterward, while Cousin Margaret called one after another of her acquaintances over to meet the "long-lost heir." Madeline derived a certain amount of malicious amusement from his discomfort, which compensated, in part, for Colin's earlier triumph.

Cousin Margaret Treadbill belonged to Grandfather's generation, and was my cousin but no relation to Madeline or Colin. She was a Charleston anachronism: after a Grand Tour made when she was a girl, she had returned to her native town and never again went further afield than Sullivan's Island in the summer. She had made herself scarce when my parents died, not surfacing until she had assured herself that Abner Mountain, with less claim on the orphan waif than she, had taken over my upbringing. Thereafter, she had been happy to house me upon my brief visits to Charleston, and she had been willing to undertake the responsibility of chaperone to Madeline when she made her debut the year following Colin's disappearance, in exchange for which she had found in Madeline the source of much entertainment and gleanings of gossip about Saramount.

I knew that Colin was aware of the importance his presence had given her little party tonight, and in spite of his irritation, was amused by it. It was just as well—Cousin Margaret's frank, unabashed pleasure bridged the gap between him and Madeline, which had begun to show signs of strain.

The street vendors awakened me the next morning. I heard the first call from the direction of the dock where the shrimp boats unloaded their catch.

> Ro-ro swimp, ro-ro swimp!
> Ro-ro-ro-ro-ro-ro swimp,
> Come an' git yo' ro-ro swimp!

Then closer at hand, almost under my window:

> Porgy walk, porgy talk
> Porgy eat wid knife an' fawk!
> Porgie-e-e-e-e-e-e-e!

The morning breeze stirred the net curtains at my window, and I buried my face in the pillow, trying to shut out the plaintive, wailing song, but it was no use. I was awake, and Rose was to be met today.

Rose, at twenty-nine, was so much like the exquisitely beautiful seventeen-year-old I remembered that I picked her out of the docking crowd at once. I was too inexperienced to recognize that the illusion was gained by every artifice and cosmetic device available to women, but the end result was perfection. And how paltry were Madeline's and my attempts to approach her in perfection of form, clothes or beauty!

We were late. The *Carolina Queen* had already discharged its Charleston-bound passengers before we arrived. Rose, waiting with superb confidence in a little sea of luggage, was attracting the attention of every person nearby. Her traveling costume was stunning, and spoke of Paris in every well-tailored line. Of azure silk, it was embellished across the bust and shoulders with little turquoise spangles that trembled and sparkled with every quick breath she drew. Her lovely face was framed by a picture hat of matching silk, mounted with a gorgeously feathered pair of aigrettes. She had the red hair of her clan, and the waves dipped and swirled about her face, with two little curls nestling on her neck.

When she saw the two red heads so like her own approaching, she dimpled. Her décolletage was just short of being indecent as she leaned forward and extended a gloved hand to Colin, who was striding ahead.

"Victor! You have become so remarkably handsome that I am enchanted to have given in to Uncle Abner's entreaties and come home!"

"It is Colin, cousin, and I, too, am enchanted that you have come home."

"*Mon Dieu!*" Her face paled to a chalk white and she drew in a sharp breath, the spangles quivering. "Colin! But Colin is dead! There is some mistake—it is impossible! The cable—the strange cable—from Uncle Abner—do you mean it was true, after all?"

"Yes, Rose. I am Colin, and I am certainly very much alive."

She had made a quick recovery and was eying him with

narrowed suspicion. *"Non, non,* you have an English accent! You are *not* Colin."

"I have been away for twelve years, Rose. Long enough to pick up any sort of accent. I might say that you, yourself, have acquired a slightly foreign one."

She tossed her head impatiently. *"Non.* I have always spoken with a continental accent. But you—I am skeptical. You can't be really—you. Although, is it possible? You are certainly a Mountain. You could be Uncle Abner himself as a young man. No one can mistake that look. You *must* be Colin!" She caught the wondering stare on my face and made a moue of apology. "Forgive me," she said swiftly, "this is heavy conversation for the moment of my arrival. I did not believe the cable, but now I see I was wrong to assume it was a trick. Do you remember, Yves, I told you that it was nonsense—no one returns from the dead after twelve years! But it seems that I was mistaken."

We had already noticed that she was not alone. He was quiet, smilingly watching Rose, as though he found her extravagant gestures amusing. He was posed against the shifting, sweating, hurly-burly laborers of the port, and in contrast, he seemed clean, shining and beautiful. Cupid, not the fat baby with the lovers' arrows, but the angelic suitor of Psyche's bridal bed, would have suffered by comparison. Blond, golden even, with slanting blue eyes and a face as innocently fresh as a child's. He was of a slighter build than Colin, but he looked sinewy and fit. Like Colin, he was dressed in white linen, and he carried a wide-brimmed Panama hat. Standing alone, with a knowing smile curving his lips, he attracted the attention of every feminine eye present. Together, as a foil for Rose's beauty, they were a matchless pair.

"It is Yves, cousins, Yves de Saussois. He is my traveling companion. I do hope Aunt Lucy can find room for him at

Saramount, for I would be desolated to be without him."
She might have been speaking of a pet puppy. "Yves, I
make you known to my cousins, Madeline—and Sarah, is it
not? Take notice! Do not practice your Parisian naughti-
ness on this little one, my pet, for she is too young for you!"
I wondered if Yves, who was apparently French, spoke our
language. Rose soon enlightened us. Leaving the mound of
luggage without a backward glance for Shand to cope with,
she moved toward the barouche, explaining that Yves, like
herself, was an expatriated American living in Paris.

With our additional passenger, we made ready to return
to Saramount. Shand and Colin, anticipating the luggage,
had already hired a wagon, but there was a short delay, and
when they returned, Colin prepared to sit beside Shand.
But Rose insisted that there was room, so we all five
crowded into the barouche, Rose placing me beside her because, she said, she wished to make the acquaintance of her
little cousin Sarah. She soon had me shyly and warmly confused by her compliments.

"We go on from Saramount to New Orleans for the
balls," she said, unfurling her parasol, "and I think we
would like to take this child with us, eh, Yves? I would
adore putting her into her first ball dress and accompa-
nying her. It would be your first, wouldn't it, my pet?"

I nodded and murmured something unintelligible about
my debut.

"St. Cecelia's? Bah! What is that? I speak of a truly in-
ternational party, and a set of people such as your little
eyes never dreamed of beholding! If Uncle Abner agrees,
then it is settled." She turned aside to her companion. "Do
you not agree, Yves? Would Sarah not be a success in New
Orleans?"

He had been watching Colin, but he obediently slanted

an oblique look at me, and nodded smilingly. In spite of my flattered pleasure at being singled out, his eyes and Rose's praise made me uncomfortable. I looked at Colin appealingly. He was sitting with his arms folded in implacable silence, but I knew that he was disapproving. So did Rose.

"I daresay we can add another to our entourage?" she said slyly. "Eh, Colin? Are you angry to be left out? Because of Sarah? *Or me?*"

Grandfather and Aunt Lucy were waiting for us on the veranda when our carriage made a sweeping entrance before the front door. Rose was enfolded lovingly in Grandfather's arms and he dabbed at a few tears that had sprung up.

"My dear little girl," he laughed shakily. "You look so much like your mother."

Yves bowed gracefully to Grandfather and apologized for his unexpected arrival.

"Your young man is welcome, of course." Grandfather smiled indulgently at Rose.

"But he is not my young man, Uncle Abner. He is merely a friend, but one whom I have grown to depend upon, haven't I, *petit?*" She looked around carelessly. "Where is Papa?"

"He is waiting for you in your room," Aunt Lucy replied. "Sarah will show you the way."

Rose shrugged as she followed me upstairs. "I must wash this travel dust off, and therefore I would prefer to wait before seeing Papa. But one should not put off unpleasant duties," she said airily. "I am sure I see him often enough —was it last year, or the year before, that I saw him all of five minutes?" At the door, she paused. "Come in with me, Sarah," she pleaded. "I want to talk to you. You've grown into a quaint little innocent. Remember what a little nuisance you were, tagging after Colin and me when we were children?"

I looked at her bewilderedly but made no reply. It seemed hard on Uncle Charles, who apparently wished to greet his daughter alone, to be forced to share this emotional moment with me. However, the room was empty; but her luggage, which had arrived before us, had been unpacked. There was hot water in the pitcher and a bar of scented soap in a dish beside the bowl.

"How pleasant," Rose murmured. "Sarah, how is Papa?"

Her question was unexpected, but I answered truthfully. "Not very happy, I'm afraid. He—"

"Never mind," she interrupted. "I don't want to know. Which is his room?"

I told her and, at her impatient gesture, began unbuttoning her dress. Thereafter, one by one, the delicate undergarments dropped to the floor, and as Rose kicked each one free, I bent to pick it up. Turning back from the bed, where I had placed the folded clothing, I saw that Rose had shed her chemise and stood naked before the pier glass, wearing nothing more than her stockings and high-heel blue glacé slippers. She was surveying her reflection with an air of thoughtful appraisal, apparently unaware of any impropriety until she saw my shocked eyes in the glass.

"Why—you're blushing, *chérie*," she said quizzically. "How amusing! How long has it been since I've seen a woman blush? My, my, it *is* an innocent, isn't it?" She reached for her dressing gown. "There, now, I'm decent! I'll spare you any further embarrassment. Now, be a pet and darken the room for me. I must have my rest before dinner. I suppose Saramount still clings to its barbaric custom of dinner at three in the afternoon?" she added.

"Yes," I replied simply.

"Don't go yet," she called me back from the door. "Before I see him again, I want the whole of Colin's story. When did he return?"

I told her everything he had told us. "A very plausible tale," she said thoughtfully when I finished. "Surely, I can't be alone in thinking—that is, didn't the rest of you assume he was dead?"

"Most of us did. *I* never really thought so. And Grandfather."

"You have no doubts now?"

"Why should I?" I was a trifle defiant.

"But, really, child! It is an ideal situation for an impostor! A slight loss of memory—a little vagueness at times—and anyone could carry it off. How can you even think he is Colin?"

"You forget his resemblance to Victor and Grandfather," I said defensively.

"*Mais oui,*" she said thoughtfully. "He was discovered, of course, by someone who knows the family well and expects to share the fortune he will inherit someday. But I, I tell you, he must be an impostor! I shall unmask him!" she added dramatically. "I promise you, he cannot deceive me —I know too much about the real Colin! He is a man— and bah! I have never seen a man yet who was not putty in my hands." She smiled seraphically at me from where she lay among the pillows and, with a negligent hand, pulled the edges of her gaping robe together. She waved the other hand in dismissal. "Now, run along, Sarah, I still have to see Papa, and for that I must rest."

But Uncle Charles did not wait for her to find him, for when I went to awaken her before dinner I overheard his voice in her room. I hesitated, shamelessly eavesdropping, transfixed by the bitter exchange.

"I demand that you send him away," he was saying.

"You are not in a position to demand anything, dear Papa."

"I still hold the purse strings, and I imagine you and that filthy little lapdog would not go far if I withheld them. Or, are you going to try to tell me he is paying his own way?"

"As a matter of fact, he is! So do your worst, Papa, you can't touch me." I could almost see the shrug of those beautiful shoulders. "But if you do, then I shall retaliate in kind, and I don't think you would like that. Saramount is not the place to begin ringing threats upon my head. I have nothing to hide in my relationship with Yves. Apparently, you haven't met him yet. I suggest you do so before passing judgment! But let us have no more threats about money, darling Papa! Our bargain was that you would supply me with all that I need, without intimidation. I don't wish to remind you of the sordid details of that bargain, but if you force me to, I will. That and more."

There was a long silence, and then Uncle Charles said brokenly, "Rose, I cannot bear this—change in you. This unkindness."

"Really, Papa, this slavish humility does not become you," Rose said disdainfully. "Behave like a man. You are among a tribe of them—Mountain men—my mother's people, and I would like to see you measure up. My poor little Yves is quite out of his element, but I expected better of you."

Another long silence, and then I heard a sound that set my skin prickling. Sobs. I crept silently away.

For the rest of that day and the following one, Rose kept the promise she had made me, and herself, and attempted to discover the truth about Colin. She had said that she could determine if he was an impostor; she had intimated that any man was an open book to her. I do not know if she was successful or not. I do not know if Colin saw through her pretty deceits and silken traps or not, but he seemed to enjoy her company, which, during this period of mourning, was apparently an amusing relief.

At the end of that time, Rose abruptly abandoned the chase, whether from boredom with an unworthy opponent, or simple frustration, I do not know, but as she arose to go upstairs after supper, she turned to Grandfather and coaxingly begged for the use of the barouche, with Shand to drive, for a trip to Charleston the following day.

"I promised Yves we would go," she explained. "He has relatives in Charleston he wishes to visit."

Grandfather could not refuse his pretty niece anything. "It sounds as though your young man wishes you to meet his family."

"You will persist in thinking of Yves as my young man, Uncle Abner," Rose replied sweetly. "I tell you again that he is merely a good friend. We are traveling companions only."

"In my opinion, a woman's traveling companion, if she is unmarried, should be a duenna, not a young man who is not related to her," Grandfather said carefully. "I don't understand it otherwise, and neither does anyone else. If he traveled in another—er—relationship, I might not approve, but it would be more comprehensible. I don't think you are aware, coming back after a long absence, that you take a chance on your reputation, which seems foolish merely for the sake of a traveling companion who serves no other purpose!"

Rose listened to him in growing amusement, and at the end threw back her head and laughed. "Oh, Uncle Abner, you dear old turtle! Did I say he served no other purpose? But he does! He and I—we—er—complement one another, Yves and I!"

Victor jerked his head up and glanced quickly at Grandfather, who was still looking stern and disapproving, then
at Colin. It was like watching twins, to see their similar
faces wear, in turn, the same variety of emotions, passing
from startled comprehension to repugnance and shock.

CHAPTER 7

The house had settled down with a series of snaps and creaks to a reluctant nighttime stillness, but I was still awake. I had crushed my pillow and dampened it with my tears; I had tossed and turned, and wretchedly fought my dragons, only to finally yield them their victory and abandon sleep.

At the open window I received the blessed coolness of the night breezes upon my fevered cheeks. Directly below me the muted sound of voices and the dim glimmer of light aroused me and turned my thoughts in another direction. I felt a stab of anxiety. Someone was in the library, and if it was Grandfather, still up and awake, he might be ill.

But the hissed, angry voices that grew more distinct as I flew down the steps were Madeline's and Victor's. Not Grandfather, after all. Both of them were so furiously angry that neither one heard me when I stopped short of the doorway. The oil lamp, its wick turned low, was on the table between them as they bent over it, their faces almost touching, glaring at one another. Victor was partially dressed, his nightshirt thrust into breeches, and wearing evening slippers. Obviously, he had been to the stables to see to the new foal, and Madeline had stopped him as he came through the open window. She was in a thin, filmy gown and peignoir, and her figure was outlined in the lamplight, but I doubt if Victor noticed that or much else in his rage.

"—go to Colin for sympathy," he was saying, "but I have none. I am no longer interested in you or anything you have to say!"

"I have tried to explain, Victor," she replied violently, "but you won't listen!"

"And why should I, Madeline? Oh, I don't blame you for feathering your nest—any woman alone, in your circumstances, could not fail to do so. I merely criticize the rapidity with which you made the changeover from me to Colin! However, in your case," he added insultingly, "speed was essential. You are, after all, no longer young and—"

"I hate you, Victor Mountain!" she gritted. "And don't dare speak to me like that! If I am still a spinster—at my age—whose fault is that, pray? And have I ever thrown it up to your face? You know I care nothing about 'feathering my nest,'" she added contemptuously, "or about Saramount. It could be razed to the ground for all I care! And as for Colin, how can you accuse me of being interested in him—"

"Because, my dear Madeline," Victor replied with silky sarcasm, "as soon as he arrived you made a brazen attempt to fix his interest. A pursuit so obvious, so pointed—you were a veritable honeybee alighting on a jam pot, with new clothes, new personality, a new *sparkle*—all designed to attract the new heir. He is a liar and a scoundrel, but he can't be blamed for accepting the lure that was thrown to him. I cannot condemn him for his part in the flirtation, for last night's tryst in the summerhouse—"

"It was not I, last night," she panted. "I swear to you, Victor, it has not been I for days now, ever since I realized how you felt. Since that night we went gigging and I stopped you on your way to your room. It was then I discovered that you had misunderstood my motives for attracting Colin. I told you I had hoped he would let something slip, become careless, if he thought I was in love with him."

"And did he?" Victor asked smoothly.

"No, of course not. He is not a fool!" she snapped. "*I* have been the fool—to think he would not see through me. You know I have never loved anyone but you, Victor." Her voice broke pitifully.

There was a long silence. He was gazing at her frowningly. She was beautiful in the lamp glow, her hair a tousled cloud around her head, her eyes dark and brilliant with tears, as she gazed pleadingly at him. Finally, he said slowly, "It could be only that you see he is interested in Rose now."

But she caught the note of uncertainty and said eagerly, "No, it is not that, Victor. I swear to you—it never went beyond a flirtation with us, and it stopped instantly when I learned that you had misunderstood my motives." She came around the table and touched his arm tentatively and, when she wasn't rebuffed, pressed herself against him, winding her arms around his waist. "Victor, haven't I proven I love you, again and again?" she murmured, raising her face to his. "Give me a chance, now, to show that I love you. Don't put me away—I am pleading, my darling—"

He saw what I saw, a face suffused with emotion as her lips blindly sought his. He bent his head and I heard him mutter "Madeline" in a strangled voice.

I backed away hastily and came up against a hard body just behind me. My startled gasp was bitten off halfway as one hand clamped over my mouth, the other around my waist, and I was dragged backward under the shelter of the stair curve. Remembering the gigging spear, I struggled wildly until Colin's whispered, "Quiet, little fool!" silenced me. In any case, Victor and Madeline were in no mood to be peering into shadows or questioning half-inaudible sounds, as Victor swept up the stairs, Madeline in his arms.

In the library, Colin faced me with an unrepentant grin, his brown eyes sparkling with mischief. I studied him by the light of the lamp which, though admittedly dim, was bright enough to allow me to detect no embarrassment at Madeline's disclosure that she had been using him. Instead, he was looking decidedly pleased with himself.

"You evidently don't mind losing your girl, but then, it didn't take you long to find a replacement," I snapped.

"Quite so," he agreed smugly.

"So the summerhouse is the trysting place, eh?" I went on. "Quite sylvan for our cousin Rose, I would have said. Not her style, I would have said. I should have imagined that she would prefer a Parisian lovenest, or a small hotel off Fifth Avenue," I added nastily, "than the rural charms of a summerhouse in the moonlight." I was being insulting, and I knew it, but jealousy had made me indiscreet.

"I prefer the bucolic, myself." He eyed me consideringly, leaning forward across the table on one hand, as Victor had done, the other resting casually on his hip. He was still dressed as he had been at dinner, but was without his collar or tie and his shirt was loosened at the neck. "It seems that I erred in the proper attire, however," he added coolly.

I blushed and moved several paces back from him, but he laughed.

"My dear little cousin," he said wickedly, "do you know that lamp shines right through your nightgown?"

A gasp escaped me, and with a swift movement I leaned forward and blew down the chimney. It took a few moments for my eyes to adjust to the dim shapes and shifting shadows outlined palely against the window, so that when he spoke at my shoulder I realized that he had taken advantage of the darkness to come quite close.

"Since you prefer the dark—" he said roughly and reached for me.

What overtook me then had all the force of a whirlwind storm and the power of a lightning bolt: it lifted me right out of myself, blanking my mind and leaving me limp, shaken, chilling and burning simultaneously. His mouth covered mine hungrily, ruthlessly parting my lips beneath his probing tongue, and I lost all sense of time or place, all sense of decorum or of my state of undress, or even of responsibility for control of my actions. He raised his head and spoke once, in a thickened, exultant voice I hardly recognized—"By God, I knew it! I knew it would be like this!"—before his mouth greedily took possession of mine once again.

As for me, I was returning kiss for kiss with all the innocence and fervor of a primitive child. My mind was blanked of everything but the thought that this was Colin —Colin, whom I had loved forever. It did not occur to me to set brakes on our lovemaking: I was mindless, lost in a thousand tactile sensations.

It was not until his exploring fingers dropped the shoulder of my gown, baring my breast, and his mouth followed the trail of his fingers that my mind signaled danger and I whispered, "Colin."

He heard me, above the pounding of my heart and the broken words he was muttering under his breath. Instantly, his hands dropped, he released me and backed a step.

"Colin." I reached out and placed a hand on his chest. Beneath my palm I felt his heartbeat, fast and strong.

"No, poppet, no." He gripped my wrist, then released it reluctantly and backed another step.

"Colin." I followed, unwilling to have him move away from me, and I heard the deep, jagged breaths he was drawing. He moved, a match scratched, the lamp flared up, steadied and sent out a glow that showed me his face. He was pale and his eyes were black, but already he had put the width of the table between us.

"No, poppet," he said roughly. "No more. Cover your breast, my darling, for I shan't be able to think until you do." His voice held a ghost of laughter. I stared at him numbly and he leaned forward and pulled up the shoulder of my nightgown, his hand lingering at my cheek. "Now. Do you understand that scene between Victor and Madeline?"

"You mean—like this?" I asked dazedly.

"Yes. Like this," he agreed gravely.

I stared at him, seeking to understand his words. How could he liken *us* to Victor and Madeline, their lust to this painful, gloriously tumultuous emotion I was feeling? He was reading my face, for now he said gently, "It's the same, my sweet. I only regret that I did not correctly interpret their problem until the damage had been done. God knows, I had no wish to further add to Victor's agony, poor devil. It placed me in an impossible situation, once I knew. I saw only that Madeline was experienced, she sought me out, and seemed to know the rules of the game; I was as eager to find out her motives as she apparently was mine! Frankly, she was a damned fool to trade on Victor's jealousy as she did!"

My head was clearer, I was beginning to think, and now I thought of something particularly unpleasant.

"And Rose? What was your reason for Rose?"

"That hurt you, didn't it, my pet?" He grimaced. "That's why I couldn't go to sleep, you know. I kept seeing your face as it was tonight—so damned miserable! I told myself, To hell with the whole thing! I'll chuck it all! Go away. When I saw Madeline intercept Victor when he came in from the stables, and right after that you tiptoed down, I had to pull you away to keep you from being seen. A reconciliation was long overdue, and your presence would have put a constraint on it, to say the least."

"You still haven't explained what you meant by philandering Rose," I said, firmly.

He grinned. "Philandering," he jeered gently. "That's a nice old-fashioned word. I just bet you learned it in that convent you were spirited away to years ago. Not that I am complaining, mind," he added quickly. "I have no quarrel with it, or its end product, for it has kept me in thrall for days now. And the possibilities ahead are—endlessly exciting," he finished shamelessly.

I swallowed nervously. "Then, you aren't in love with Rose—"

"In love—with Rose? You can think that? It must be that damn girls' school again." He came around the table and tilted my face up to his. "You want an explanation for Rose, eh? Pure and simple, an attempt to exchange information, as it was with Madeline, and incidentally, keep you, who had already become a disturbing distraction, at arm's length. And a fine job I did of it too!" he added ruefully. "It's a game I play with redheads, my sweet. Not with little brunettes. I went into this with my eyes open, I admit that. I recognized the danger—to myself, but not to you. If I had realized, if I could reverse events—well, no one told me what you were like! I've been off balance for days now. To hell with Saramount; it's not important any more! Victor can have it—he always could. Right now it boils down to just two things. You—and an absolute determination to find out what happened to me twelve years ago! *You* aren't safe until I do, and I know damn well *I* am not."

He pushed me gently into a chair, still wondering, shaken, wanting to cling to him, yet knowing I should not.

"Now, sit there. I'll get this chair over here and we can talk." He tossed me Grandfather's afghan. "Will you do something about that nightgown, Sarah? That's better. Now we can talk sensibly. I lost my head tonight, my darling, but I don't intend to again. You are my own little poppet, just as you always have been. I admit it. But we have things to do before we can begin to think of our own future. My coming home has stirred up a hornet's nest. You can see that it has to be resolved now."

"Is it important, Colin, to know who——?"

"*Very* important, Sarah. Surely you can see that? Your Uncle Marion was murdered! It can be argued that he was an old, sick man, in pain much of the time, but you were the intended victim. *You,* Sarah! And then, there are the others. Victor and Madeline, in spite of their reconciliation, regard one another with suspicion. Grandfather sees disaster ahead. Uncle Charles——Rose——the truth *must* come out!"

"But you——and I, Colin," I started to say, driven by a compulsive need to link us together, but——

"There can be no future for us either, Sarah," he said patiently. "Remember your nightmares? And this——childish fantasy——obsession——call it what you will, about me that you've clung to long past the time to let go."

"No." I denied, shrinking back into the shadow of Grandfather's chair.

His face was pale. "Yes," he said grimly. "I won't accept a sick imitation of what can be the real thing! I think we must find out the truth, for all our sakes."

"What can *I* do?" I asked humbly.

There was a slight lifting of the sternness in his expression. He rose and strolled over to the open window, where he regarded the rolling expanse of the lawn with calculating eyes. The moon had, by now, topped the tallest pines, then sunk beneath them, leaving the lawn in darkest shadow. I heard a rustle of leaves, and smelled the sweet, musky scent of gardenias as a night-prowling animal strayed too close to the house and disturbed the shrubbery. Colin turned away, smiling whimsically into my hopeful face.

"You can think, Sarah. Reach down deep into that memory of yours and dredge up every single last thing you can. About anything."

"There's nothing more. Honestly."

He considered me. "Perhaps not. You're too tired right now, of course, to give it your proper attention, so forget it."

"You said that before. That night."

"Said *what?*" he asked alertly. "You're too tired—"

"No. To forget it—think of other things. I don't know why," I added hastily, anxious to apologize for my little fragment. "I think I had been crying, and you sat on the side of the bed and talked of other things, trying to get my mind off whatever I was trying to talk about. I knew you were trying to change the subject, because every time I went back to it, you would say, "Forget it, Sarah, think of pleasant things."

"Forget *what?*" Colin was frowning. "Something we saw on the way home?"

"Well—" I temporized. "It could have been. It's a two-mile walk. You carried my shoes," I added, irrelevantly.

"And the popcorn. Yes, I know. That's all past history. I'm looking for something more, Sarah. Perhaps—" He stopped, then went on with a cold, clinical appraisal that disturbed me more than his insistence. "Perhaps you know nothing at all, and I've been wasting my time. In the meantime, I want to ask you something else. Someone mentioned tonight something that I had forgotten. The midnight train, which is an express, does not stop in Talley unless the stationmaster wires ahead or someone is getting off. Is that right?"

I nodded.

"Then, how did I get on the train? The stationmaster didn't wire—he didn't even see me. Only the conductor, remember? I already had my ticket, of course, but the train had to stop for someone else, and there had to be some confusion, or I would have been noticed, wouldn't I? So— who got on—or off?"

"I don't know." I blinked. "Also, how did you know the train would be stopping?"

"Exactly. I think we are on to something, Sarah. Why didn't the person who got on, or off, come forward and mention seeing me? It was advertised enough, wasn't it? So why keep quiet about something so innocent?"

"Unless it was someone who couldn't tell," I replied, the answer coming to me in a flash of inspiration.

"Couldn't tell? But, my God, how big is Talley? My disappearance was a nine-day wonder—"

"No, I didn't mean that," I explained. "I am speaking of the Harrisons. Their bodies arrived that night—the stationmaster would have been expecting them! And I suppose that is how you found out about the train—you picked up the information at the carnival, as Grandfather did, or you overheard someone talking at the station." But he was frowning, and I asked puzzled, "Why? Is something wrong?"

"Yes." He sounded disgusted, and he cast a slanting, wary look at me, as though uncertain of whether to answer. "I am merely thinking what a fool I have been, not to see this before. Joe Bob has been desperately trying to talk to me for days, and I have been avoiding him. It has occurred to me that he might have been the only person not interviewed about that night. Is it possible he saw something?"

"Yes!" I said positively. "I *know* he did! He would have been at the station, and at first he would have been too grieved to listen, or even be told, about your disappearance. He said himself, he had just heard the story for the first time when you returned. After twelve years. Then he realized he knew something you should know."

"Yes." Colin's eyes were glittering with excitement. "The one person who could have helped me! We must try to see him tomorrow. Where can we find him?"

"He said he would wait for you at the Old Place," I replied. "I think, after trying to see you once at the church, that's where he will be."

"Good." He pulled me to my feet and, when he saw that I was waiting hopefully for him to kiss me, tweaked my nose. "I have a powerful urge to keep you down here with me, little one, but I know that I must not. So it's off to bed with you, and no more kisses tonight!"

And I had a powerful urge to try to emulate Madeline's behavior. I wondered if I would be able to break down Colin's resolve to send me off, if I did. But I wasn't sure at this point if I wanted to find out, so when he turned me around and headed me toward the stairs, I did as he said and went meekly to bed.

CHAPTER 8

"Do you remember the time the old bull alligator came up behind you and Joe Bob while you were swimming? You two almost capsized the boat—and me with it—scrambling into it. Grandfather would have beaten you if he'd known you were swimming this far downriver."

Colin's eyes danced. "Particularly if he'd known we'd brought you with us," he admitted.

But now Colin seemed unwilling to discuss Joe Bob, or what he might have to tell us. Since I was unable to think of any subject that did not come back to him sooner or later, I fell silent. I could see that Colin was anxious to get there: it was as though he was driven by a demon, and he rowed with quick, choppy strokes that propelled us at an amazing speed down the river. This morning he had been unaccountably exasperated with himself that he had misunderstood what I had told him about the Old Place, for when I got downstairs to an early breakfast, it was to find him waiting, and he had eyed my thin muslin frock with a mixture of annoyance and approval.

"Have you forgotten our appointment, poppet?" he asked quizzically. "Charming as that dress is, I don't think it will be serviceable as a riding habit."

"And have you forgotten that Joe Bob will be waiting for us at the Old Place?" I reminded him. "However, you may be right about riding, because if he isn't there, we will need the horses to find him."

"Precisely." He smiled brilliantly at me. "But nevertheless, stupid of me to forget. I had the horses waiting, but I'll see to their unsaddling and tell Grandfather where we're going while you eat breakfast. And change to a habit—but hurry!"

And it was the sight of the alligator, perhaps the same one, sunning himself on a convenient log, that recalled to my mind the story of Colin and Joe Bob, who had disobeyed Grandfather by swimming where they had been told not to. Unlike Colin's taut anxiety, my mood was a particularly euphoric one this morning, which, combined with our surroundings, reduced me to a state of giddy irresponsibility. I eyed Colin surreptitiously, watching the light play on the muscles of his arms as he pulled steadily at the oars. He had rolled up his sleeves, but in his riding clothes he looked hot and uncomfortable, and if he had been sixteen, would have, no doubt, commanded me to take my turn at the oars.

The morning was already hot and sultry, with a hint of a pending thunderstorm. The sun, reflecting off the water into our faces, was merciless, and mindful of its tanning propensity, I unfurled my parasol with a snap, thereby disturbing a pair of majestic ospreys, who apparently were nesting in one of the estuaries and were alarmed by the flash of color. Colin eyed me crossly and I thought was just opening his mouth to suggest that we would both benefit by the application of another pair of arms, when I interrupted him saucily.

"Don't scowl—it gets cooler just ahead." After last night, I dared anything.

The river was separating around an island and we followed the narrower channel, which rapidly passed into a shadowed tunnel created by laced branches and vines overhead. The sunlight changed at once into a welcoming, dank

coolness. Our progress became slower as Colin guided the
boat through a maze of cypresses, standing to their knobby
knees in water, and rotted fallen trunks of trees brought to
their feet by the remorseless grip of parasitic vines. For the
unwary, there were submerged stumps, waiting to snag or
scrape the hull of a boat. This was the swamp, where the
sunlight was almost nonexistent and the atmosphere retained a grayish-green haze, a subtle blending of the thick
hanging moss and the deep, black river. This was the
swamp, silent and cruel to the reckless traveler who was
unaware of its dangers.

"Why does he live here?"

Colin's voice brought my head up. I had been peering
over the sides, watching for moccasins, which have been
known to coil around an oar and drop into a boat. "There
was no other place for him to go," I said simply. "When the
county took over Dr. Harrison's property for back taxes,
Grandfather paid out this island and offered it to Joe Bob
as a home. He fishes and hunts for food. There is a Negro
family downriver who feed him when he seems to need a
good meal. At night, unless it is cold or raining, he takes a
bottle to the churchyard and sleeps there, or in the church.
At first, some people objected, but the minister insisted that
it was Christian charity to allow him that comfort. He's
harmless—everyone, even the children, likes Joe Bob."

Colin's eyes met mine. I knew he was seeing Joe Bob as
a boy, not just as a bearer of information. Once, he had
been all freckles, tow hair and impudent grin, but it had
been a long time since I, or anyone, had seen him like that.
But Colin would remember him that way.

"We must see if we can help him," he said abruptly, then
looked beyond me at the derelict, shabby Old Place.

The Old Place was precisely that, a one-room shanty
built on stilts with a shaky porch projecting out over the

water. Its origin had been lost in time. Some said it was once the home of a trapper, plying his trade along the river in the days of the old plantations, but it was probably built by a settler who lived in it for a brief season until the rising waters and swamp miasmas forced him to see the folly of its location. Once, the Old Place had been accessible by horseback, but long ago a change in the river current eroded the land until it stood isolated on its own island, away from the mainland. As a hunting and fishing lodge for Dr. Harrison, it had been satisfactory; as a home for Joe Bob, it was barely tolerable, but the only one he wanted.

"He's here," I commented as Colin tied our boat to the porch beside a moss-covered old pirogue.

Colin called, but there was no response from the house. Joe Bob was apparently asleep, and although I was not afraid of him, drunk or sober, I did not relish the thought of having to arouse him from a drunken stupor in order to talk to him. Colin must have been viewing the task with the same lack of enthusiasm, for he climbed the ladder with a resigned air. A minute later he was back, leaning over the porch railing.

"He's not home. Come on up." He held out his hand.

In spite of its unsteady underpinnings, the porch was sturdy and, from its appearance, was where Joe Bob spent most of his time. Coiled rope, cane fishing poles, floaters and a shrimp net cluttered the floor in untidy heaps, but in contrast, the cabin's one room was painfully clean and neat. The bed was made, its coverlets tucked tightly in sailor fashion under the thin, skimpy mattress. The table had been set with a clean plate, cup and spoon, and the dishpan, its rag wrung out and left to dry on the rim, had been hung up behind the little potbelly stove. Under the window, an upended wooden box served as a cupboard, holding his few pitiful supplies and a frying pan and coffee pot. The one oddity in the empty, waiting room was provided by a note which had been started on a sheet of ruled notepaper, left on the table beside the cup.

"Dear Colin—" Joe Bob had begun in an unsteady scrawl. That was all.

My eyes filled with tears. "I want to cry," I faltered.

Colin looked around the room again and his face sharpened with sudden urgency.

"There's something wrong!" he said savagely. "God—am I too late? I don't like any of this—the way this place feels! As though— Let's get out of here, Sarah, and find him. *Now*."

We were descending the rickety stepladder before I traced the source of my own uneasiness. "Why is Joe Bob's pirogue still here?" I asked. "He hasn't any other way to get off the island, unless he swims."

"Or—unless someone takes him off," Colin agreed grimly. "Come—let's don't waste any time."

"Do you have any suggestion where we might look first, Sarah?" he asked while we were waiting for our mounts to be saddled.

"The church," I replied promptly. "Let's try there first."

As we approached the church, however, we saw that something was wrong. The doctor's buggy, recognizable by the black bag that reposed forlornly on the empty seat, told its story first, and then we saw the group of men who were standing apart, glancing apprehensively over their shoulders.

"There's been an accident," I cried, but when Colin's eyes met mine, I knew he didn't believe it, any more than I did. The doctor would not have left his bag in the buggy to deal with an accident, and we both knew that only one person would have been in the churchyard this hour of the morning.

By this time, Traveler and Nellie had brought us, all too soon, upon the scene. The lifeless body was lying on the ground, but only the stiff sprawled legs were visible; the sheriff and the doctor, squatting beside it, concealed the body from our view with their bulk.

"Is it Joe Bob?" Colin called and the sheriff jerked up, then rose from his kneeling position.

"It's Miss Sarah, isn't it? And that's Colin?" He peered at us. He was a large, grizzled man, with faded-blue eyes lost in a seamed, tanned face. He had been sheriff for years, but I knew that Colin would not remember him, so I introduced them.

"I knew you were back, of course," Sheriff Tate said quizzically, "but I haven't been out to see you. I've been waiting for Abner to notify me when you were ready to talk to me. I figured when you remembered something I should know, you'd be calling on me." He patted Traveler's arched neck with a caressing hand.

Colin ignored the reference to himself. "Is it Joe Bob, Sheriff?" he asked impatiently.

"I'm afraid so, Colin. There's no use trying to keep it quiet in a place this size. It is going to cause a lot of activity among the ghost hunters, happening as it did in the churchyard. They'll be seeing the poor fellow's ghost for the next fifty years," he added wryly.

"Then—he's dead?" I faltered.

"Yes, Miss Sarah, I'm sorry, but he is." The sheriff's shrewd eyes were sympathetic. "Why don't you dismount and walk over to the spring, ma'am. Get yourself a drink of water and get a grip on yourself. This is no place for a woman right now."

"No!" I slid obediently off Nellie but clung desperately to her flanks. "I won't go," I repeated stubbornly. "I want to know what happened."

"Well—" he looked at me doubtfully. "Joe Bob had a heart attack sometime during the night, brought on by some sort of seizure. He was killing himself, of course, on moonshine liquor. A sheriff of a county as big as this one can't run down every still that appears in the swamp. As fast as one is destroyed, another springs up—" His voice trailed off peevishly on what I suspected was an old grievance.

The doctor called to him, saving him the necessity of further justification, and he hurried back to his side.

Colin's hand gripped my elbow. "Let's walk the horses, Sarah," he said in a low voice. "There's something wrong about this, and I want to speak to the sheriff again. Have you observed the doctor? He is worried about something and his examination has been a lengthy one for what is merely a heart attack. I don't think he is satisfied with his own diagnosis."

Colin looped our reins over the branches of a gnarled wisteria vine, then stood so he could watch the scene behind us.

"What sort of man is that sheriff, Sarah?" he asked urgently. "Is he as stupid as he seems?"

I didn't answer. I was trying grimly to concentrate on something other than the sounds going on behind me, the doctor's orders, then the shuffling footsteps as Joe Bob's body was carried to the waiting buggy. And I kept seeing the clean little cabin, and the poverty of its meager furnishings. And poor Joe Bob's legs, outstretched toward us. There had been a hole in the soles of both shoes. People had tried to help Joe Bob—friends of his parents, Grandfather—but it had been useless. Apparently, the blow of losing his parents and Colin at one fell swoop had been too much. He had not wanted help from anyone, only to be left alone to kill himself at his own pace.

The sheriff had returned now, solicitously bearing a dipperful of water for me, and he watched me benevolently as I drank. Both men were apparently taking my weakness for granted, and they were taken aback by the crispness with which I demanded further news.

Joe Bob had been poisoned. I thought at once of Uncle Marion, and the narcotic used in his coffee, but the sheriff had not received any hint of an association with Uncle Marion's death from the doctor. The doctor was sure of his facts, however, and judging by the odor from the half-filled bottle under Joe Bob's body, the poison was to be found in it. Joe Bob might be killing himself, mused the sheriff, but his was a slower method by way of bad liquor, and this was murder. Therefore, in view of recent stories Joe Bob had been circulating about Colin, he was very interested in our explanation of what might have happened.

"We heard all about it, although he was cagey, as drunks are, saying that what he had to tell was for Colin's ears only. He was waiting for Colin, he'd say."

Colin was pale. "Those stories reached our ears too," he admitted with disarming innocence. "But Sheriff, I wouldn't put much faith in Joe Bob's drunken meanderings, if I were you. I didn't. True, we were looking for him— Sarah and I just left the Old Place, but it was for the sake of old times, not because I believed he had anything important to tell me."

I looked at him wonderingly, asking myself why he was lying. Was he afraid to bring the investigation—an official one, this time—back to Saramount's door? The sheriff, however, apparently accepted his explanation in good faith, and made his goodbyes with a courtly courtesy that sat oddly on the big, rough-looking man.

On the way home, Colin was deep in thought, but I, too, was not eager for conversation when I thought of Joe Bob's weak, loose grin. Perhaps Colin was thinking of that, or of the sheriff's last words before he sent us on our way: "Well, we won't know anything much until we know what poison was used, so it's too early to jump to any conclusions. I'll do a little investigation around here, but in the meantime, tell Abner I'll be out to see you folks later."

It was almost dark before he came. By that time, the storm that had been threatening all day had descended, bringing thunderclaps, lashings of rain and lightning, and had passed, leaving much cooler air behind. Grandfather, complaining querulously of the dampness, huddled before a fire. Rose and Yves arrived just ahead of the storm, excited and laughing, only to have their laughter stilled as someone told them about Joe Bob.

The sheriff was blunt, and his invitation that everyone was to meet him in the library was a thinly veiled order. Any lingering thoughts that one might have about suicide were dealt with summarily. Joe Bob had been murdered by an enormous dose of strychnine introduced into the liquor he was drinking. It would have been an easy task for the murderer, for Joe Bob was in the habit of hospitably pressing his bottle upon whatever companion he was with. But most damning was the fact that there was no way for Joe Bob to have obtained the strychnine on his own.

"It's a fairly common poison, Sheriff," Uncle Charles objected gently.

"For you folks, yes," the sheriff turned to him. "But you forget how limited his life was. He had no money, and what he had went for liquor. He existed solely on handouts and charity. He hadn't been out of town for years. And I learned today that the only poison sold in Talley is rat poison containing arsenic. So, unless someone gave it to him and he put it in his own bottle, it is murder."

"I see," murmured Uncle Charles reflectively. "You *have* been thorough. He did, indeed, live a restricted life."

"Very restricted," the sheriff agreed ironically. "But the most conclusive proof was found at the Old Place." He turned to Colin. "You didn't mention that his pirogue was still there, tied to the porch. Without it, he couldn't have left the island on his own. You see, he was a creature of habit. About ten or eleven o'clock each night, he would row across the river, tie his pirogue to the dock of his nearest neighbors, a Negro family, and pass their house, singing, headed for the church. I talked to them about it today, and they said that recently he has broken his habit— he has been staying at home, and last night was no exception."

"Which means—?" Colin asked.

"Which means that he had to be transported by boat across the river, and it docked somewhere else. We might find it, if we were to look, tied in underbrush somewhere, or perhaps floating downriver. It happens all the time. Did one break loose from the dock at Saramount last night, Abner?" His eyes flicked toward Grandfather. "He was staying at home for one reason." The sheriff turned back to Colin. "He was waiting for you. Evidently, he had begun a letter to you when someone arrived last night and offered to take him to you. Perhaps, even, with a message from Colin, which would have certainly lured Joe Bob from home. On the way, perhaps, he was offered a drink, and once he had begun, poor Joe Bob would have found it impossible to stop." The sheriff smiled grimly. "That's one version. The other is simpler. *You* were the person he wanted to see—if you'd shown up, he would've broken off his letter and followed you wherever you took him."

Everyone was shocked to silence by the direct accusation. "Does that mean you are accusing me of murder?" Colin finally asked in a deceptively gentle voice.

"No-o-o," the sheriff replied consideringly. "Merely giving one version of what could have happened. So far as I know, you were the only person he was interested in. Why? Did he know you for a fraud? I've heard the rumors, the questions that everyone is asking. People wondering—are you really Colin?" The sheriff sounded mildly curious. "What does the family say?"

Colin smiled engagingly, directly into the eyes of his inquisitor. "It's more to the point, in the present case, surely: What did Joe Bob say? I admit I have my detractors, but there are others who accept me for what I am. It occurs to me that I misjudged you this morning, Sheriff," he added sarcastically. "You have spun an ingenious case out of air —something I did not suspect you capable of doing."

I was tempted to speak, seeing that Colin had no intention of defending himself, but Colin checked me with a flickering, warning look. Why was he refusing to offer the sheriff the theory we had settled on last night? It was only one explanation, but a good one, surely. And it would certainly divert suspicion from him. But the answer came back to me with overwhelming logic: if Joe Bob's jealously hoarded secret was the identity of Colin's attacker, as we had assumed, he would never have gone with him last night. Besides, no one else had known that we planned to question Joe Bob today. Reluctantly, I remembered Colin's strange behavior this morning—particularly, his strained anxiety to reach the Old Place. Who, then, was this man? This Colin? Could he have killed Joe Bob? No! But I was not equally sure that he was not a stranger. I felt dizzy as the beloved face shifted, seemed to dissolve and change into a double-faced shadow man.

"I don't suppose you have an alibi for the early hours of

the morning? Say, from midnight until about two?" the sheriff was asking stolidly.

Colin laughed. "Sheriff, would that be likely? Only two of the people in this room have alibis, to my certain knowledge," he added casually.

A startled silence greeted his words. Madeline looked wildly from Victor to him. "I suppose you mean us?" she cried defiantly. "If you do, speak out. I am not ashamed to admit that we were together all night!"

"And if anyone questions the proprieties," Victor growled, "then let me assure you that we intend to be married as soon as it can be arranged."

"Married?" Aunt Lucy rose unsteadily to her feet. She did not notice, as I did, Madeline's equally startled reception of the announcement. "Married? To that hussy? That —that harlot?"

The sheriff colored to the roots of his grizzled hair, but more was yet to come, a stream of vitriolic abuse that was largely incoherent. It was as though the public announcement, long dreaded and now a reality, had loosened the weakened gates to Aunt Lucy's sanity and control, and she concentrated her hatred on her enemy, going back into Madeline's childhood for every fragmentary incident that seemed to indicate a depraved character or an abandoned pursuit of her son. Her words, which were as battering as a physical onslaught, left her victim—nay, us all—stricken dumb until she came to a panting, disjointed stop.

By this time, Grandfather's head was hidden in his hands and the sheriff's face was a study of hideous embarrassment. Victor was huddled in an armchair, flinching as his mother's voice rose and fell in her passion.

It was Colin who put an end to it. Stirred by Victor's white face, he rose briskly and put a firm hand on her shoulder. "Come, come, Aunt Lucy, that's enough for now." His eyes swept the room, passing over Yves contemptuously and settling on Uncle Charles. "Uncle Charles and I are going to take you to your room. You are tired and need to rest. Sarah, you'd better come, also."

Aunt Lucy looked at him dully. I don't think she recognized him, but with docile obedience she allowed the two men to lead her from the room.

The sheriff did not linger, under the circumstances, nor was he long in sending the doctor, who ordered Aunt Lucy tied to her bed, as he talked vaguely to Victor of an eventual cure. But he sounded hopeless. "She must be confined at once, tomorrow, before she harms herself or Miss Madeline. I'll arrange it with the hospital."

I was limp with tiredness by the time he left, and in no mood for Paulie's vagaries when she came to my room to help me dress for supper. She had been pressed into service by Victor and had been an interested spectator to the doctor's visit.

"She stiff as a bo'd, Sarey. Doan' even know Mistah Victah, it seems lak. Doctah Mueller says she'll kill Miss Mad'line if she gits a chance."

She was trembling and seemed acutely uneasy. "Don't worry." I cocked a cynical eye at her. "Mister Victor won't ask you to sit with her."

"Oh, Ah knows that! He says it's his job an' no one else's."

So that wasn't it. Yet Paulie was not herself, she dithered about my dressing and wrung her hands and finally snarled the comb in my hair. I confronted her bluntly.

"Something's wrong with you. What's the matter?"

There was no use being anything but blunt with Paulie: to be subtle was to lose oneself in the byways of her own muddled thinking. It had always been thus with her. She had not changed from the giddy, silly youngster who had brought me to Saramount as a baby and thereafter drove a humble, adoring Shand distracted by her fickle nature until she finally put him to rest by marrying him.

"It's them!" she gasped, her eyes rolling at me appealingly. "Shand say, he say—tell Sarey. He say tell Sarey they's somethin' wrong wit' them. Shand say—tell Sarey she ain't to have nothin' to do wit' them. Tell Sarey to go her way an' let them goes theys!"

I was frowning, trying to puzzle through her words to the message Shand had obviously sent me. "What are you talking about? Didn't Shand explain? Sit down, Paulie, and try to tell me just what he said."

Paulie seated herself reluctantly on my bed, and I turned away from my dressing table to face her. The light fell directly upon her face: it was racked with desperation. She took a deep breath and plunged ahead and I saw that she was making a noble attempt, for once in her life, to keep to the point. "He say fo' me to tell you. He say he know he shouldn't, 'cause she's mebbe to marry Mistah Colin, an' Mistah Colin mebbe boss heah someday. He says he knows Sarey must be tole, 'cause he heared her, invitin' you to go to one of them far-off places—"

"Oh. That." By now, I understood that Paulie was referring to Rose, but I had forgotten her invitation to take me with them to New Orleans. So much had happened since that day when, firmly convinced of Colin's indifference, I had been willing to consider leaving Saramount. "Oh, Paulie—stop worrying. Tell Shand to stop worrying. I won't leave with her."

She sighed and her words came out gustily. "I'se glad, Sarey. Shand say ef you start to, he is goin' to Mistah Abnah heself! He says they's somethin' wrong wit' them two."

I tossed my head, very woman of the world, and turned

back to my dressing table. "Shand is old-fashioned, Paulie. Miss Rose calls him—Mr. de Saussois—a friend, but— However, things are different in Paris."

Paulie looked skeptical. Paris meant nothing to her. It was not her place to judge Rose's relationship with Yves either, but she saw that I had misunderstood her, and she struggled to make her meaning clear. "Ah ain't talkin' about thet, Sarey," she said dryly. "Shand say when they goes to Charleston, he drops them off at thet hotel on King Street—th' one yo' gran'papa won't let you walk past. He say whin he goes back fo' them, he talks to th' po'tah, an' th' po'tah says them two goes upstairs wit' *two* men, one fo' him, an' one fo' her!"

Paulie's eyes met mine in the mirror. Rose's wantonness was, by this time, no secret to any of us in the family, and what the family knew, the servants knew. But this—this was different. Remembering Rose's words to Grandfather, her light dismissal of Yves as a lover, I knew a glimmer of the truth, as much, I am sure, as Paulie did, although it was as vague and unnatural to the two of us as the sexual practices of the Eskimos or the Hottentots.

"Don't say any more, Paulie. I don't want to know any more!"

"Yes'm." Her duty done, Paulie rose and began to capably brush my hair. Her face wore a closed look, and I wondered what she was thinking.

I wore a sprigged muslin with a sweeping skirt, and my mother's cameo pinned to a black ribbon around my throat. I felt in need of reinforcements, for it seemed that everyone was wearing a mask; that deceit, evil and lust lurked behind the faces that smiled across the supper table.

Briefly, for a minute only, Colin had time for a private word with me before supper.

"What's the matter?" he asked hurriedly.

"Rose and Yves." I stopped, unable to continue.

"What have you heard?" he asked urgently.

"Shand told Paulie to tell me—" I couldn't bring out the ugly words.

"Damn!" He looked savage. "It would seem that she owes her mother's blood the decency to keep her foulness away from Saramount, at least!"

It was another unhappy meal, with the air crisscrossed with suspicion, irritability and distrust. My eyes continued to stray toward Rose, in spite of my resolution to avoid her, and it seemed that she was paler than usual, and her light, inconsequential chatter was stilled tonight.

In the end, it was Grandfather who contributed the final horror of the day. "I could pity Joe Bob," he began abruptly, breaking an uncomfortable silence. "If I had room in my heart for pity. But I have not, for Joe Bob died as he would have wanted to, and in the place he loved best in the world."

Everyone had started at his introduction of a subject that we had been studiously avoiding all evening, and when he finished, we continued to stare at him blankly, unsure of the meaning of the strange sentiment he had expressed.

Finally Colin, in the manner of an actor responding to a cue, answered him. "And you cannot mourn him, sir?" he asked tentatively.

"No! I mourned Colin, but I do not mourn Joe Bob." Grandfather surveyed us grimly, with a surprising insensitivity to our shock. "Am I alone in that? Did none of the rest of you brood over Colin, and where he might have been?" His eyes swept the table. "When we thought him dead, did none of you think of him, our good, beautiful boy? Was he forgotten so easily? Was it only my nightmare, to know that Colin was buried somewhere, alone, unmourned, abandoned by those who loved him?"

The shock was complete, but now it was laced through with terror. Rose stood up, stumbling, and put out a protesting hand. "Don't! I can't bear it—"

In a vain attempt to wipe the horror from her face, to soothe her trembling body, I cried out in a loud, silly voice, "But—but—Colin's alive, Grandfather! How can you— you mustn't distress us with such talk—"

Grandfather's eyes looked directly into mine. "*Is* he, Sarah? Is he, really, alive?"

CHAPTER 9

I stood in the doorway and whispered as though I was in the presence of the dead or dying, nervously avoiding the sight of Aunt Lucy tied securely to her bed. Her eyes were open, fixed with a blank stare at some point beyond me.

"She quiet now, honey," Mammy reassured me calmly. "Mistah Victah ast me to stay wit' her aftah I cook breakfus. Thet Paulie, she no good a'tall!" she added dryly. "A chile'd be mo' he'p than her."

"You look tired, Mammy," I said worriedly.

"Ah ain't tired—least, not lak Mistah Victah. Now, *he* mighty sick-lookin' this mawnin'. Ah spec's th' doctah'll be heah pretty soon. Go git yo' breakfus, Sarey. Nath'n's keepin' it hot."

But Nathan had let the flame go out under the coffee and grits, leaving them a cold, gelatinous mass. And I soon learned that no one at all was downstairs. I could have even believed that the house itself was empty, except for Mammy and me, and her patient upstairs, but I knew that Rose and Yves would still be asleep. An explanation could be given for the others, but I was alarmed by Nathan's absence, knowing that only one reason could account for it: Grandfather. Remembering his cold, withdrawn silence since learning of Joe Bob's death, his strange words last night, which had seemed so unaccountable to the others, I was touched by a sudden frenzy of nervousness and dashed wildly out the kitchen door, calling loudly and sending the hens into frantically squawking circles. But the kitchen yard was empty, as were the stables and barn. Something was wrong—something that couldn't be explained by a domestic crisis, or even Aunt Lucy's breakdown.

Then I heard the sounds, coming from the direction of the south lawn. A shrilling, tearing noise that resolved itself, as I ran toward it, into the screech of ripping wood. The floorboards of the summerhouse were being torn up. I recognized some of the stable hands, and all of the house servants, among the circle of onlookers who, as I approached, shifted and parted for me to push my way in.

Most of the floorboards, except a few on the outer circle, had been already pried up and stacked to one side, and a deep hole was being dug in the exposed dirt flooring. It was one of two holes that had been dug, but the other had been abandoned. I made out Shand and Victor, who were bent over their shovels, carefully raising one spadeful of dirt after another. Colin hung over them, leaning on a pick, but he had had his turn, for he was hot and sweat-stained and, in wiping his brow, had left a smear of dirt across his cheek.

One of the summerhouse benches had been placed to one side, and Grandfather was seated on it, his hands and chin resting on his cane as he bent forward, watching intently. Madeline huddled beside him. Grandfather looked ill: his eyes were black with pain and the flesh around his cheeks and mouth had shriveled until it was clinging to the bones. Nathan, who had been watching him anxiously, touched his shoulder hesitantly, and Grandfather reached up and absently patted the trembling black hand.

I ran forward and, kneeling before him, peered anxiously into his face. He made an obvious effort to greet me normally. "Sarah, my dear, why are you here? Go back to the house at once."

I turned to Madeline for an explanation and was shocked by her trembling lips and her eyes, suffused with tears. "What's the matter?" I demanded. "What is Victor doing?"

Colin glanced around at the sound of my voice. Before I knew he was there, he had jerked me roughly to my feet. "Sarah," he said sternly, "you mustn't stay here. Return to the house. Now!"

"I won't!" I cried. "Why should I? What's going on? What are you doing?"

A shout from Victor interrupted us, and Colin reluctantly loosened his hands and placed me on the bench beside Madeline.

"Shand has struck something," I heard Victor mutter. "This may be it."

A swelling murmur broke from the onlookers. Colin knelt at the edge of the hole. "Can you tell what it is?"

"No. Not yet. Take it easy now. It's rotten." There was a scuffling sound as Victor and Shand carefully stood up, holding an earth-encrusted object between them. "My God"—Victor sounded stunned—"I never believed we'd really find anything."

"It had to be there," Colin said briskly. "It looks like the valise."

It might have once been a valise, but as they laid it carefully upon the ground, it was not recognizable as such. I stared at it blankly. I was loathsomely rotten and had burst open upon exposure to air. Colin pried at its contents with the tip of his pick. There was a flash of metal: I gasped, and Colin, with a sharp look at me, turned back and used his finger to probe.

Anyone could see what it was then. The tarnished silver buttons and that portion of the sleeve which had been folded under, with the school patch sewn to it, were in recognizable condition. Colin's school blazer.

"Is there anything else?" Grandfather asked in a trembling voice. His eyes were wearing a blinded look.

"Just a minute, sir, and we'll see." Victor sounded subdued. I heard Colin say, in a low voice, "It has to be here. Nothing else fits."

"Mistah Colin, suh, can you take ovah fo' a minute?" Shand's voice was shaking.

"Yes. Perhaps I'd better." Colin scrambled down to take Shand's place. By this time the stillness was breathless, for it was obvious that the two men in the hole were expectant. Then we saw them jerk as their spades struck an object: the two heads, so alike, bent over, but it was Victor who scrambled out and stumbled to the edge of the summerhouse, where he slumped to the ground, shivering.

I gazed at him wonderingly, then back at Colin, who remained crouched out of sight. I looked at Grandfather and saw that tears were trickling slowly down his cheeks.

Abruptly, Colin leaped out onto the ground and walked over to us. His face was set and stern, but otherwise, he seemed untouched by the emotion that had racked Victor, Grandfather, even Shand.

"I think, sir, that you might want the area cleared, and perhaps wish to withdraw yourself, before we go any further," he said stiffly, refusing to meet Grandfather's eyes.

"Then—it is him?" Grandfather implored Colin.

Colin swallowed and said nothing. Grandfather looked toward Victor. "Victor—is it him?"

Victor had his back to us and he didn't look around. "Yes, sir, I think so."

"Who?" I cried. "Who are you talking about?" My voice rose to a near scream. Colin gripped me with steel fingers as I started to run forward.

"Tell her," Grandfather said sternly. "She has to know sometime."

"It's Colin, Sarah," the man who was restraining me said. "Colin is buried there."

"What are you talking about?" I shrieked. "*You* are Colin!"

"No, I'm not Colin," he said sadly. "I have never been. Colin has been dead and buried there, under the summerhouse, for twelve years. I think, perhaps, since soon after he said goodnight to you."

I screamed then. Higher and higher. It was my nightmare repeated all over again, but this time with no hope of awakening to a saner, kinder world, no Grandfather to soothe me, and promise and reassure me that someday Colin would return. I saw the ring of shocked black faces around me, and the anguished eyes of the man whom I knew as Colin, and my scream bubbled in my throat. He jerked me into his arms and held me against his chest, but as soon as I felt that familiar body against mine, I turned into a biting, scratching, clawing animal, desperate to get away. He loosened his arms and I fought my way clear.

I ran toward the swamp. Instinct, and some small prompting of caution, guided my footsteps so that I avoided the quicksand, the cottonmouth moccasins and the alligators. I ran until I found a small hump of slightly higher ground where I could rock, bent double, and nurse the pain tearing at my vitals. I ached with hurt and misery, and the swamp creatures avoided me, as they would have avoided a wounded one of their own kind.

I do not know how long I remained there, for I did not feel hunger or any of the normal discomforts that might have brought me out of my grief, but it was, nevertheless, a very human emotion that eventually intruded itself upon my anguish, and then, finally, drove me to my feet and started me home. Curiosity. I might, and did, hate him, but

I had to know: Who was the man who had impersonated Colin?

From the sun, it was high noon as I approached Saramount. I cut a wide swath to avoid the summerhouse: I hoped never to have to look at it again. I was muddy and streaked with muck and grass stains, and my shoes had been sucked off my feet, so that I was barefoot, but I went directly to the library and stood in the window.

It was dim, after the bright sunlight outside, but I could make out Grandfather and Victor. Victor was standing in the doorway, his hand on the knob, preparing to leave, and at his exclamation, Grandfather turned around. I ran to him, sobbing, and flung myself in his lap.

"Sarah." He stroked my hair gently. "It is a hard blow for you. You've lost him twice."

"Sarah, where have you been?" Victor sounded subdued, unlike his normal, aggressive self.

I ignored him. "Grandfather," I asked, raising a drenched face, "was that truly Colin buried in the summerhouse?"

"Yes, my dear," he said gently. "We must accept it now, you and I. He is dead."

"Then, someone killed him and put him there?"

"There is no doubt of that either," he agreed.

I shuddered. "Was it that man who—pretended to be Colin?"

He was surprised. "Why, no, of course not, my child! Is that what you've been thinking? You are confused, dear. Colin was killed twelve years ago."

"But who is that man?"

"Who is he?" Grandfather said cautiously. "He is a friend of mine, Sarah. His name is Jack Ransome. He did this impersonation at my urging. Mine, Sarah, and no one else's. I had a difficult time persuading him to do it, but I knew that I must. When I first saw him and realized how much he looked like Colin—yet wasn't Colin—I knew that it was right for me to use him this way, to find out the truth."

I stared into Grandfather's eyes. They were defensive, slightly wary, as though he was unsure of my reaction to his confession. Funny little images seemed to dance behind them—visions of Colin or Jack popping into the library to speak to Grandfather when he was unsure of where we were going. The Old Place, for instance. And Rusty. Of course Jack would know, for Grandfather himself had been the only person to know! Belatedly, I recalled that Grandfather had warned me not to fall in love with Colin, because he might be a stranger. Sudden tears welled, I blinked, and they became Grandfather's familiar eyes again, gentle and kindly.

Victor had not left the room. "Sarah," he said humbly, "you look dead on your feet. Would you like some food— and some tea?"

"A very good idea, my boy," Grandfather said briskly. He eased me gently into a corner of his chair and stood up. "We're in somewhat of a muddle today, my dear. There won't be any dinner, for the doctor hasn't picked up his patient yet, and Mammy is remaining with her. Victor is incapable of any firm action, and the women have taken to their rooms with crying spells." With steady hands, he carefully measured out a portion of brandy in one of the bell-shaped glasses. "For you, I think you need a restorative. As for me, I have not felt so at peace in years." He smiled slightly.

I took the glass. "But why did you let me think Colin had come home? Why didn't you tell me the truth?"

He kept his back to me as he carefully stoppered the decanter. "Yes, that was cruel," he agreed regretfully. "I did warn you, you know. But believe me, I had to do it. There was no other way. In order to convince the others, you and I had to believe in Colin, and I'd do that, and more, to flush out his killer."

Victor returned, carrying a tray with a pot of tea and two enormous, slablike roast beef sandwiches. I was touched, for I could see that he had made them himself. He pulled up a table carefully and looked at me anxiously.

"I apologize for the meal, honey, but no one was in the kitchen to help. Not even Madeline—she is prostrate in her room. She insisted on staying until the end, this morning."

"What about Rose?" Grandfather asked.

"I'm sorry, sir," Victor said hesitantly. "But she says that she and Yves are leaving tonight. There is a nine o'clock train for New Orleans. I know you won't like it, but she insists that she won't stay under the present conditions."

Grandfather's face darkened with anger. "She can't leave! Colin's and Joe Bob's bodies will be at the church tonight, and the family *must* be there to receive sympathy calls from old friends. I've arranged for the funeral to be early tomorrow, and private. She has to stay through that, then she may leave. This thing isn't settled, finished—there must be an end to it soon. Come, I'll talk to her! Jack?" He looked over my shoulder. "Sarah needs someone else now."

"Yes, sir." He had been standing behind me all the time, but he seemed oblivious to my indignation as he dropped easily into the chair vacated by Victor.

"Do you mind if I stay with you while you eat, Sarah?" he asked smilingly.

Suddenly conscious of my appearance, I tucked my bare feet under my muddy hem. "You might find it more pleasant elsewhere," I said carefully. "This room is rather warm this time of day—"

"Thank you," he replied blandly, "but I find there is enough air circulating to be quite comfortable."

I scowled, but manfully chewed my bite of sandwich. And then, he chose that moment to upset my precarious balance.

"Was it such a terrible day, poppet?"

My chin quivered and I put my sandwich down quickly. He leaned forward and took my hands gently in his. "I'm sorry, my dear, that I had to be the one to tell you the truth, but you had to know. I was well into this charade before I learned of little Sarah, and even then, I had no idea of the effect her coming would have on me. How could I have known what my emotions would be when you threw yourself into my arms? And what could I do then but continue as I had begun, and hope to retrieve myself in the end?" he added with gentle irony.

"But I don't understand any of this," I complained, pulling my hands away and gripping them nervously in my lap. "Why, after all these years, did Grandfather decide to put us through this? And if he knew where Colin was buried, why go through this—this charade—bringing a stranger in—"

"Hush, Sarah, my girl!" he scolded me softly. "Knew where Colin was buried, indeed! Don't you listen to people? Of course he didn't know! But your grandfather left you here with me, so that all these answers should be forthcoming. I will satisfy every question when you finish your luncheon—*if* you can. Those sandwiches of Victor's look as though they were made for a stevedore," he added in an amused voice.

"You sound as though you know something about the sea, after all." I muttered.

"Of course. Those stories I told you about my sea voyages were true, only slightly altered to fit the case of Colin.

Then, when I grew tired of roving, I took my share of the family inheritance and settled down on a farm, with horses. But not in Canada. That story was given to explain my English accent. Rather, would you settle for Indiana, my love?" he asked coaxingly. "A rather prosaic ending, I am afraid, after the swashbuckling adventures I spun for everyone's benefit, but true, nevertheless. A farm in Indiana, Sarah—and a good life."

"Then, you were born in England?" I murmured with a fine show of indifference, brushing aimlessly at a stain on my skirt.

"In Surrey. I will show you the house—my oldest brother's home—someday, when this is all cleared up and we can proceed as planned with our future," he added, casually.

"But you must see that it is all different now," I began.

"Can it be that you are trying to jilt me?" he mocked tenderly. "After assuring me in this very room the other night that your intentions were honorable?"

"I was talking to Colin then," I cried indignantly. "You are *not* Colin."

"No, because he is dead, and has been for twelve years, and the sooner you accept it and stop crying for a ghost, the happier you will make your grandfather, not to mention me and a few other people," he snapped. It was the first anger he had shown me since our conversation began, and I, wanting sympathy and consolation was taken aback. I glared at him, wondering how he could speak as though I was at fault, the wrongdoer instead of himself. By inferring that I was a source of worry to Grandfather, by touching upon my concern, he knew that I could be depended upon to respond with all the quivering speed of a trout rising to a lure.

"Finish your tea so that I can put your tray away," he

said roughly, ignoring my scowl. "I can't talk to you while you're chewing and I certainly can't kiss you, and I have every intention of doing both! So let's get on with it. Do you prefer sitting in that big chair all by yourself, Sarah?" he asked irrelevantly.

"Yes," I replied oppressively.

"Very well. It's your loss. Then reach behind you and hand me that notebook on the table. Before you came in, your grandfather was showing it to Victor. I, of course, saw it some time ago."

"What is it?" I handed him the stained little booklet.

"It is, I suppose, a diary. It was brought to your grandfather a year ago by one of the carpenters doing some repairs to the underpinnings of the house. It had been hidden away there for years. He tells me that after he read it, he walked the floor for nights, trying to decide what to do." Jack riffled the crumbling pages reflectively. "He had known for a long time that something must be done—about Victor, mostly. Although he was sure that Colin was dead, he could not, would not, pass the succession of Saramount on to his murderer, and without any clue to who he was, he was at an impasse. But he realized he was being unfair to Victor. And the others—their problems, though hidden, were there, complicated by the mystery about Colin. But finally, there was you, Sarah. You are your grandfather's special love, my darling, yet you had never accepted the fact of Colin's death, and he was afraid you never would. Most importantly, he feared for your safety when you returned to live at Saramount. He had kept you away for years, fearful that your nightmares betrayed a special knowledge that was dangerous to you."

But he never told me! And for those years, I had wondered why I wasn't allowed to stay at Saramount. I remembered that first Christmas away from home. I had been eight years old, and sick with loneliness. There had been an enormous tree in the equally big, echoing dining hall, and we few who were left, staff as well as pupils, had rattled about like jangling peas in an empty jar. I was inconsolable in my misery, and had cried all of Christmas Day, longing for Grandfather, wondering why he had sent me away. A tremendous surge of sadness rose within me for that little girl, and equally, determination to discover the person who had done that to her. It was too late for her now. But what had Grandfather said: "I'd do that, and more, to flush out Colin's killer!"?

Jack was reading the emotions in my face very well and he began to eagerly talk about the diary now. "We don't know who wrote it, or even the writer's sex. See what *you* think."

I reached for it quickly, resolved to find some clue they had overlooked, and opened the first page. The writing was round and stumbling, reminding me of a child's first attempts at lettering. It was the same childlike scrawl on the last page as on the first, although it soon became obvious that the diary covered a period of several years, and there was nothing childish about its contents. As I read it, I was struck by its somnambulistic quality, almost as though it was written in a dream (a particularly bad dream), but the notion being a new and strange one to me, I dismissed it instantly because of its lack of probability.

I read the first page twice, in growing disbelief, and thereafter, skimmed the pages rapidly as my revulsion increased, until I came to the final shocking page.

"today a baby came to saramount only colin could stop her crying the others do not know but colin is not a good person he is bad bad tortures babies animals too i have even seen him doing it i hate him hate him hate him"

Hate! The book was a litany of hate; the word has

crooned over and over, lovingly, and no one was spared.
Abner Mountain was wicked, evil; he trifled with his black
servant girls and beat the men, his grandson, his ward
Sarah. "i would like to see roses face laid open to the bone
with a whip for she is wicked and greedy proud of herself
bad." Madeline and Victor. Here the diary lapsed into ob-
scenities as their love affair was carefully detailed. Lucy
Mountain, with her extremities of behavior, was not
spared, nor was anyone else, including the servants and me,
the baby. On the basis of elimination, therefore, it seemed
impossible to determine the identity of the writer, but he,
or she, was undoubtedly an inhabitant of Saramount. However, some were treated more gently than others. The most
virulent passages were reserved for Colin, as though this
gentle, defenseless boy had somehow aroused all the hatred
and jealousy within the dark labyrinth of a sick mind. Passages denouncing Colin seared the pages like a stream of
scalding acid, accusing him of every sordid vice this mind
could project, and undoubtedly the mind *was* knowledgeable. Until finally—Colin must be punished. The
diarist dwelt with loving detail on the method of punish-
ment, until I wanted to cry, "No more! No more!" Murder
was not mentioned; death was obviously too kind. A more
subtle method was considered, one that would hurt Colin
more than physical pain, a practical method. "it would be
easy to kill a little girl by taking her to the attic and hanging her from one of the beams i wonder . . ." Reflectively,
a thought to ponder on. Had it been easier, and more pleasurable in the end, to kill Colin himself?

I was white-faced when I put the diary down, my fingers
feeling soiled by the contact. "Who—here at Saramount—
could write something like that?" I whispered.

"Your grandfather thinks the person was not normal at
the time. Perhaps now, one would look upon the mask of

sanity and not see it for what it was," Jack added noncommittally. He slid a loose page out of the back and handed it to me. "You wondered how your grandfather knew where Colin was buried. This morning, when he awakened, he found this under the door. It could have been put there anytime yesterday and he wouldn't have noticed it last night by lamplight, he says. He noticed the similarity of handwriting at once, and aroused Victor and me before breakfast. That's why we were digging in the summerhouse so early."

It was the same handwriting, the ink was fresh, and the paper a piece of Saramount stationery. "why dont you look in the summerhouse look in . . ."

"Your grandfather thinks the diarist had a conscience about Colin. Do you remember the conversation at supper last night when he deliberately introduced the subject? He did so, hoping for some sort of reaction." Jack added carefully, "He thinks the message was put under his door last night."

I read it again. Wasn't it a bit taunting, a subtle mockery of an old man? I was swept with revulsion. "Then it wasn't Aunt Lucy?"

He took the paper from me. "We can't be sure, although of course Victor has leaped at that possibility. He is frightened. Also, why was Colin buried at Saramount when he was killed elsewhere? Unless it was because it was the one place where they wouldn't search," he added reflectively.

I looked at him cautiously. In spite of his mild, judicial weighing of the evidence about the book, I could see that he was exhausted. His face was drawn, and his eyes wore a haunted expression. It had been easy to forget; in fact, Jack encouraged one to forget that he was a stranger, yet upon him today had fallen the task of bringing up the body, having it identified, notifying the sheriff, and performing the many other details that I was sure no one else had been capable of doing, all completed while I had been cowering in the swamp. Had I contributed to that look of strain? I could honestly admit that I had been resentful of him; even, irrationally, blaming him for not being Colin. It had not been Colin but Jack, I remembered suddenly, who had made love to me the other night.

"Jack," I said warmly, "if you are not too tired, will you tell me how Grandfather discovered you?"

He sat erect, blinking, and cast me a wary look. Heretofore, I had not been friendly, and certainly not sympathetic: he had expected to have to fight every inch of the way to retrieve the ground he had lost. He rightly interpreted this slight shift in his direction as an encouraging sign, and already he was looking brighter, fresher. "Do you remember the trip your grandfather made last year for new stock?" he asked briskly. "Victor was ill, and it was his first trip in years."

"Yes."

"He met me there. We were at an auction at a famous training farm in Kentucky. He first attracted my attention by his marked staring, so that when he finally walked over and introduced himself, I was in the mood to snub his impertinence. But he disarmed me by begging me to forgive his rudeness, and asked me to indulge him further by providing him with a bit of my background. I was intrigued," he added whimsically, "for it was an unusual opening gambit for a confidence man. So I obliged him with my history and, as I talked, I could not mistake the emotions that ranged over his face: disappointment, sorrow, relief and, finally, a reluctance to let me go. He asked me to have dinner with him in his room later, when he would explain his odd behavior, and since he seemed to be a courteous old southern gentleman, I agreed to go. Particularly after he insisted that I make inquiries about his credentials from the auction officials. Also, unless one has feminine companionship at these affairs, one can be rather bored in the evenings," he added innocently, in the face of my startled look.

"I am sure you were not often bored," I murmured ironically.

He grinned. "No. Well, somehow, I felt that Abner Mountain's story would be more entertaining than that provided by other company. He told me later that, while he waited for me in his room, he thought up the entire scheme which he later proposed to me. His difficulty was in persuading me to consent to it. I liked the old gentleman and was sympathetic with his difficulties, but I could not leave my own interests to indulge him in such a charade. He begged me to come to Charleston for just a short while—two or three weeks, at his expense, and see if what I discovered there would not change my mind. At the end of that time, if I was still adamant, I could go." He rose and began to pace restlessly about the room. He had now reached the point where he evidently had difficulty in explaining, even to himself, his motives for beginning the deception. "It wasn't altogether the adventure," he said defensively, "although, truth to tell, a wild yarn ever appealed to me. And it wasn't the money," he added reluctantly, "for I did not need it, or want it. Not that the sum of ten thousand dollars is not a strong persuader—and at one time in my life, all that would have been needed. But now, I had my own life, with my own interests. But then he came up with an offer I couldn't resist." He gave me a shamefaced smile. "He offered me Traveler. That, plus an appeal I could not refuse." He dropped into his chair and eyed me wryly. "So against my better judgment, I came here in December and stayed in Charleston, while I drilled myself in what I would need to know to play my role. Then I returned home to await his summons in April, when Rose was due to come home."

He was finished and I mused over his story, which, in the light of what I already knew, showed how quickly Grandfather had turned chance events to his own advantage. Imperceptibly, my preoccupation was pierced by the amused look in his eyes as he raked me from head to toe. I was embarrassedly conscious of what he was seeing: stained gown, bare muddy feet, and tangled hair covered with bits of twigs and pine straw. I flushed and his smile broadened. "As a matter of fact," he drawled, with a twinkle, "I intend to deprive him of a far more precious possession than Traveler when this thing's ended."

CHAPTER 10

A pall was lifted from the house by the removal of Aunt Lucy. Victor's brow cleared and Madeline came tentatively out of her room, her headache on the way to disappearing. The doctor's wagon, bearing two stout female attendants and a driver—so many, for the quiet, docile creature she had become!—had just rumbled down the drive and out of sight, when the sheriff arrived. He wanted to learn what arrangements Grandfather had made for the funeral, but his real purpose was to inform him of the doctor's findings. The body had been positively identified as Colin's and the autopsy had shown his death to have been caused by a heavy bludgeon, which, with a single blow, had fractured his skull. Death would have been instantaneous, Grandfather was told, thereby relieving a secret fear he had nursed for years.

But I did not learn any of this until later, for it happened while I was in the library with Jack, an interview that went on and on, and would have lasted indefinitely if we had not been interrupted by Grandfather. It had been a difficult day for an elderly man—with more, and possibly the most painful interval at the church, yet to come—but I was struck again by the mood of peace and serenity that seemed to buoy him, and continued to aid him in bearing each new blow and disillusionment.

I did not see any of the others, however, until we met in the dining room at a hasty, thrown-together meal concocted by Mammy—early, since she and the other servants would be expected at the church with family. Everyone was present but Rose, who apparently had every intention of carrying out her earlier threat and leaving at nine o'clock, shaking the dust of this house of mourning off her feet, and facing the headier delights of New Orleans.

Uncle Charles, who evidently had been told of her decision, looked stricken. I was reminded that I had not seen him since yesterday, and I was shocked at the change that had occurred in him overnight. I could not be sure that any of it had come about because of the discovery of Colin's body this morning, for he simply wasn't interested in the desultory conversation that followed, when Grandfather told us the results of the autopsy. And his had once been the clearer brain, the most decisive, pithy comments! Now he ate, drank, raised his napkin to his lips, and moved like an automaton, with occasionally a slight wandering of his eyes, as he looked toward Rose's empty chair with an agonized question. Had I wished to be fanciful, I could have likened Uncle Charles to my nightmare version of Colin.

Throughout the meal, to the accompaniment of rustling skirts and pattering footsteps, Paulie passed through the dining room, on her way from the kitchen to Rose's bedroom upstairs and back again. Carrying first her ironing over one arm, then a handful of frothy undergarments to be rinsed out, and finally, bridling importantly, she fluttered directly under Nathan's wrathful face with a tray covered with a white napkin. Each trip had brought a glowering frown to Grandfather's brow, and it was obviously only a question of time before one of the two elderly men reached an explosion point.

It was Grandfather who finally called her over to him with a quiet ferocity and twitched the cover off the tray.

"She say she jes want tea an' burnt toast, Mistah Abnah."

Paulie tossed her head, apparently unaware of the icy disapproval with which Grandfather glared at the contents on
the tray.

"Leave that here and tell her I want her downstairs immediately."

He was speaking with unusual restraint, but this was not
Uncle Charles. Even Paulie picked up the frigidity in the
atmosphere, for when she returned a minute later, she attempted to sidle past without stopping. Grandfather lost his
temper. Within seconds, he had her reduced to tears, an
easy accomplishment, but one that never failed to drive
him even further into distraction.

"She say she packin'," Paulie bawled. "She doan' have
time to come down! She leavin' soon, she say!"

"No!" Grandfather stood up in a towering rage, his hair
a furious white aureole, and slammed an angry fist upon
the table. Paulie wailed and fled. He turned on Uncle
Charles and Yves, his eyes blazing. "I have had enough! I
don't know which of you has the most control over that
woman upstairs, but I insist that she come down and make
an appearance at that church tonight! *We will,* I say, go together and sit as Colin's family, while our old friends come
and express their sympathy! If the murderer sits with me,
that is a matter for his conscience, not mine! Those pitiful
bones in that closed casket will not care, for he is long past
that. I have mourned him for twelve years, and my Sarah
has mourned him twice, but tonight, and tomorrow, I expect my family to be with me when I put him decently to
rest. In the meantime, I tell you, whichever of you has in-
fluence with her, get Rose downstairs, or I will choke her
into submission."

He had quietened, but his voice was threatening with
heavy menace. Yves, his face ashen, rose and scampered
upstairs. No one of us spoke, for we were listening to the

muted sounds above: a knock, followed by whispered voices, then finally, soft, hesitant footsteps pattering on the stairs. Rose was coming down alone.

Grandfather met her at the foot of the steps. The rest of us followed, in the manner of spectators following a drama, but Uncle Charles remained alone at the table. He had listened passively, without a change of expression, to Grandfather's furious burst of rage, and he seemed equally ⸻⸻⸻⸻ ⸻⸻⸻⸻ ⸻⸻⸻⸻ pearance.

⸻⸻⸻⸻ ⸻⸻⸻⸻ even, I think, to Grandfather, but ⸻⸻⸻⸻ ⸻⸻⸻⸻ see that he found it so. She was ⸻⸻⸻⸻ ⸻⸻⸻⸻ rying for a lengthy time so that her ⸻⸻⸻⸻ ⸻⸻⸻⸻ d coarse, and streaked with thick ⸻⸻⸻⸻ ⸻⸻⸻⸻ d powder. Her eyes were swollen to ⸻⸻⸻⸻ ⸻⸻⸻⸻ ly pressed a damp, wadded hand- ⸻⸻⸻⸻ ⸻⸻⸻⸻ e talked.

⸻⸻⸻⸻ "I don't expect you to understand, ⸻⸻⸻⸻ ly cannot go to that church and sit ⸻⸻⸻⸻ you seem to wish me to. Colin and ⸻⸻⸻⸻ ple coming in, staring at us, talking ⸻⸻⸻⸻ , Uncle, but it is physically impossi- ⸻⸻⸻⸻ . You ask too much. Please let me ⸻⸻⸻⸻ n."

⸻⸻⸻⸻ wait until after the funeral. For my ⸻⸻⸻⸻ respect and the love you had for ⸻⸻⸻⸻ lded sternly.

⸻⸻⸻⸻ ot do," Rose sobbed. "I refuse. You can't force me to remain. I can't. I can't."

He sighed. "Very well, Rose," he said heavily. "I see that you are near breaking point. Remain here, in the house, tonight; compose yourself, and attend the funeral tomorrow. Then you may leave, the three of you, your father and . . ."

"No!" Rose gasped. "No! I want to go tonight. Yves and I

are leaving at once. Papa may stay if he wishes, but I am leaving tonight."

"If you leave like this, before the funeral, you will never be allowed to return to Saramount again." Grandfather was watching her closely.

"I don't care! I don't intend to come again. I cannot bear death—funerals—I am sorry, but I shouldn't be asked to endure such unhappy things. I was fond of Colin, truly, I was, but this is asking too much of me. I was pleased to come too." Her eyes found Jack. "Why couldn't you have been Colin? Why did it have to turn out this way? It was such fun for a few days! No, Uncle—I cannot endure unhappy things, sad things . . ." Rose clung to the railing, her eyes filling with tears.

Grandfather's eyes did not waver from that stained, quivering face, no longer pretty now, no longer his enticing little niece. "I can see you are to be pitied, my girl," he said heavily. "What is to become of you? After your father is gone, who will care about you? You can't skim through life like this, always taking from people, never giving anything of yourself! Don't you know that someday there will be a reckoning?"

She was paper-white. *"Don't!"* she whispered hoarsely, "Don't talk to me of growing old, Uncle. I shan't ever grow old. Before that happens, I—I—will—I know ways that are painless and easy—"

"Hush, woman, that is blasphemy!" Grandfather roared. "I never expected to hear one of my kin speak such words in this house!"

"Forgive me, Uncle Abner," she said nervously, appeasingly, "I think if my mother had lived, I might have been different. But it is too late now."

"Is this why your father is a walking ghost? Is this what

has turned him into a living dead man? Your selfishness, greed, debauchery, indecency—"

Such words would have flayed me like a whip, I would have crept away in shame; but Rose took them without a single flicker of her eyelid betraying that they meant anything beyond a slight surface scolding. Instead, she summoned up a trembling, flirtatious little smile as she begged, cajolingly: "Please don't fuss so, dear old Uncle. I can't help it if I must avoid unpleasant things. Please—puh-lease forgive me!"

Grandfather glared at her in disgust. Then turning away, as though he did not wish to look upon her face any longer, he threw back over his shoulder: "Very well, Rose. You and your silly young man have my permission to leave— the sooner the better."

Her face changed, grew prettier, as though a mask had descended. Within seconds, her eyes were sparkling and the tear tracks seemed to disappear before our eyes. She passed over Madeline and me indifferently—apparently, the New Orleans scheme had died even as it was born—but she had a roguish moue of regret for Jack and Victor, as though loath to leave two attractive men.

"Did you hear, Yves?" she called gaily upstairs. "We may go! Darling, we have been rescued! I knew my naughty old uncle would not make me do something so unhappy. I must be surrounded by pretty things, pretty people, or I will die."

"Pretty souls, Rose?" Grandfather asked ironically, turning back for a moment.

A shadow passed over her face. "How old-fashioned and quaint, Uncle Abner. Souls are out of fashion in Paris nowadays!"

"I suspect no more so than they are here, Rose. For your sake, I hope you never discover that you have one. Now, run along, don't keep that young man waiting. He is your kind of person."

But Rose had already turned and was flying upstairs, pausing only long enough to call back over her shoulder: "We must hurry, if we're going to make that train!"

Grandfather turned away sadly, his eyes discouraged, and looked at us. "I am sorry," he said simply to Uncle Charles. "She is my niece, and I loved her mother very much, but she is doomed." He held out his arm to me. "Come, my love, and let me hug you. I find that I need my good children with me tonight." He extended the other arm to Madeline. "Never mind. The rest of us will be together to pay our last respects to my boy tonight. Jack, will you see to it that a hack is sent out from town for Rose?"

"Gladly, sir."

So we did as Grandfather asked, and went together to the little church, and Rose had been right: it was too hard to bear, yet was borne. For me it was a test of endurance, of sadness of spirit and sheer physical discomfort. I wore my black challis with its heavy trimming of satin and velvet; Madeline's second-best black hat, from which the feather had been ruthlessly stripped and a veil substituted instead; and my new ankle-high, buttoned shoes. The stiff wooden pews built by my great-grandfather were hard, and pressed into my spine the little buttons that marched down my backbone. They were also very narrow, and the winter challis showed a distressing tendency to slide on the polished wood.

The flaring oil lamps on the communion rail lit the pulpit and, behind it, the carved, wooden replica of the great Royal Seal of England. It had saved the little church in Revolutionary times, when the countryside was overrun by British soldiers, and its colors glowed just as richly now, in the subdued light, as they did then. Beside it was the memorial window erected by my great-grandfather, the same who was responsible for the pews, and I found that by staring steadily at it, or alternately, the King's Seal, I could avoid looking at the two pathetic coffins banked with flowers.

The insects, the moths, mosquitoes and fireflies, attracted by the lighted lamps, fluttered in and sang around our ears. There were the flowers, too, filling the vases and lining the communion rail—wild flowers, garden flowers, ferns and, lastly, the roses, lavish and heady with perfume. I shall always remember the cloying fragrance of the roses.

We sat together as Grandfather had said we must, the family and the older servants who had known Colin: Nathan and Mammy, Paulie and Shand, Aunt Carrie— who had been Grandfather's nurse, was ninety if she was a day, yet sat ramrod straight for all of the two hours she stayed—and Willie, who had taught Colin to ride.

The people came in and murmured words of sympathy. Some stayed and others went away. Among them was Mr. Thatcher, Colin's and Joe Bob's teacher. He had once said Colin was the brightest pupil he had ever had. Another was old Dr. Simpson, who had encouraged Colin's interest in medicine. There were many others who spoke of the boys, and how fitting it was that they, who had been such great friends in life, should—and here the voices broke and trailed off, leaving the obvious ending trembling in silence.

Throughout it all, I watched Grandfather, who endured this long, barbaric, cruel ordeal with stoic fortitude, and I knew that the visitors who came and pressed his hand and murmured a few words did so under a compulsion as strong as the one that kept Grandfather and Aunt Carrie rigidly in their seats.

When Jack came in and bent over Grandfather to whisper a few words, I knew this was what I had been waiting for. Grandfather beckoned to me, and I rose stiffly. "Go with Jack, Sarah. Do as he says. I will see you later."

Jack's hand under my arm was steadying as we walked toward the door. I could see the curious looks sent our way, but no one spoke or stopped us. I am sure these people were confused to see this man, whom they had lately regarded as Colin, wearing a black armband and escorting a member of the family he had, so far as they knew, duped.

In the doorway we were stopped by the sheriff, who tipped his hat to me and exchanged a significant look with Jack. "You'll call me if you need me?" he said and, at Jack's nod, stepped back to allow us to pass out into the cool, sweet-smelling darkness. The churchyard was rimmed with waiting wagons, buggies and tethered horses. A small campfire had been built in the center to ward off insects, and people stood around it in groups, quietly talking. Our appearance hushed the voices, but no one stopped us as we made our way through the crowd to the road.

We were out of their hearing before Jack explained.

"Will you be able to walk home barefoot, Sarah?" he asked anxiously.

"Is that where we are going?" I asked with serene indifference.

"Yes, back to Saramount. I want you to take off your shoes." He bent and knelt before me, tugging at the buttons of my shoes which, without the aid of a buttonhook, were stiff and difficult to manage. As he worked, he talked. "You see, my girl, we are in the midst of a memory test. We are going to duplicate every single thing we can about that walk home with Colin. I suggested it to your grandfather and he and the sheriff seemed to think it was worth a try. I even have the popcorn." He pulled a bag out of his pocket and waved it under my nose. "This is our last attempt, for our little group of suspects is breaking up. Aunt Lucy is gone; Uncle Marion, Joe Bob—God help them; and I watched Rose leave a few minutes ago with Yves. Charles will undoubtedly depart in the morning. It is a sad little game, hardly worth the playing, but we must see it through, perhaps for no other reason than to reassure ourselves at the end that we have done everything possible."

By this time he had my shoes off and I removed my stockings, tucking them into my beaded reticule. I felt rather cautious about going barefoot in the dark, but Jack was steadying me, and the relief, after the rigid, confining shoes, was immense.

Going barefoot, wriggling one's toes in the dust—what other conscious act brings childhood memories so quickly to mind? It had been a wise decision on Jack's part, to duplicate this part of my walk, for with this encouragement, I found myself easily remembering that night.

Jack was talking. "Empty your mind of every thought but that you're a little girl again, Sarah, and you're walking home from the fair. Your heart is sore because you don't want Colin to leave tomorrow. You're a little jealous too." Jack might have been practicing mesmerism, so soothing and hypnotic was his voice. I nodded dreamily.

"Is that true, Sarah? Did anything happen while you were walking home?" he was saying insistently.

"Nothing happened," I responded agreeably.

He drew in his breath sharply. I sensed that he was disappointed, and I was touched that I had not been able to say what he expected. "But you did meet someone on the road?" he asked.

I thought a moment. "No."

He was silent, baffled by my negative.

The moon was lost among the tangled branches and I was back in my nightmare. Soon, I felt. we would enter that room at Saramount again, and I would see— I reached out desperately for Jack, and he gripped my hand reassuringly.

("You're shivering, Sarah."

"Because I'm cold, Colin."

"And because your forgot your sweater! Here, take mine, and next time remember your own, my girl!")

I was confused and looked warily at Jack. Had I actually been talking aloud to him as though he was Colin, or had I merely dreamed what had been said? He seemed to be unaware of any oddity in my behavior, so apparently nothing had been said. "We're here, Sarah." And we were—on the lawn of Saramount. Already? I felt frightened, ill, as though I had lost a great gap of time. I had really been mesmerized, as surely as though I was a performer on the stage. Nothing else would explain this light-headed feeling, this strange sense of floating airily, as though time had stood still, or was meshed into the past and the present.

"Is it the same as it was that night?" Jack was asking in a monotonous voice, and I realized, with a start, that he had been repeating himself.

I looked at Saramount. Something was different.

"It's dark," I complained, sounding childish even to myself. "Someone should have left a lamp lit."

"Do you mean that a lamp was lit that night?"

But now I could not remember, although a moment ago I had known.

"Was the light upstairs or downstairs, Sarah?"

If someone had come home before we did, wouldn't there be a light upstairs in a bedroom?

"Where do I leave the popcorn, Sarah?"

Ah, I knew the answer to that. That was easy. Popcorn belongs in the kitchen.

At the door to my bedroom, Jack waited for me to light my bedside candle while he hovered uncertainly on the threshold, holding the lamp. He was disappointed, uncertain and irritable, and I felt that all those emotions were directed at me, who had so outstandingly failed to perform as he expected. He was still talking, but I managed not to listen by a simple method of shutting my ears to his voice. Suddenly, he swore.

"Damn the conventions," he snorted and strode roughly into the room. He sat down upon the bed and pulled me down beside him. "Think, damn it, think! We haven't come up with a single thing so far. Is it possible—can it be—that nothing happened, that we've all been wrong and you saw nothing at all?" he added, incredulously. "Put your mind to it, Sarah. What did Colin do right at this moment?"

I looked at him doubtfully, feeling guiltily like a prima donna who has been placed upon the stage and has failed to perform. Obediently, I tried to please him. "He poured the water into my bowl and washed my feet," I said in a singsong voice, like a parrot repeating by rote what he has been taught. "He undressed me and put on my nightgown. He laughed because Mammy had put two petticoats on me. She always did the first of September, heat wave or not. He sent me to the water closet and waited until I came back. He was going to read me a story."

"Was he wearing his sweater?"

"No, I don't think so. Why?"

Jack hesitated. "The buttons—found with him—he was wearing it when he was buried."

Suddenly it did not seem like a game any more, but a serious, frightening reality. It had been Colin who was murdered, and I felt a dizzying wave of sickness and buried my face in my hands, shuddering. Jack sighed and put his arm comfortingly around my shoulders. "I know, poppet. I don't like forcing you, but you must try again. Was there anything else?"

"Nothing," I replied dully. "Nothing that I have not already told you."

He looked at me speculatively, his eyes curiously dark and unreadable. "For the first time, I am beginning to believe you are right. Perhaps we are all wrong, and it happened *after* he left you."

"Jack?" I gasped. "Can you mean that you thought I saw Colin murdered?"

"We all thought so," he said defensively. "Your grandfather and—"

"Oh. No, *no*. I did not realize—then, that's why—" I stopped. Shaking my head violently, I added, "If that's what you think, you can put it out of your mind. *I know* I didn't see Colin murdered."

He watched me curiously. "And you seem positive, for the first time. I believe you are right, although I can't imagine, otherwise, why you were a target for murder. Well"—he stood up abruptly—"I shan't worry about you any more, love. Perhaps you saw the murderer skulking on the stairs, and it's been swept away with other childish memories. But the others are returning—I hear them—so I'll leave you now properly." He bent swiftly and kissed me lightly on the forehead.

However, at the door he turned and smiled mischievously at me, and in a near-blinding flash of recall, I saw Colin standing there. He had worn his sweater, after all, as Jack had said, and his face had been pale, his eyes filled with doubt and—yes, shock.

("Goodnight, little sister.")

I almost called to Jack to come back, so that I could tell him how I remembered Colin leaving me. But there was nothing new, and I heard him talking to Grandfather outside my door. I knew from the tired, disappointed voice in which Grandfather answered him, that he was telling of our lack of success.

I made my preparations for bed, and they were so similar to that other time, particularly when I washed my feet, that I found it easy to remember now. When I slid into bed, I knew that my candle had burned with a steady little flame, and that Colin had leaned across me to snuff it out with his fingers.

("Please, pretty please, Colin!") That was Sarah, a spoiled little minx, who never failed to coax from Colin whatever she wanted with that cajoling little phrase.

("You mustn't try your wiles on me, my girl. If I allow you to have your way now, what will I do about stopping you when you're sixteen?"

"But just a little picnic, Colin, with the popcorn. Then I'll go straight to bed and won't tease you any more. I promise."

"Very well, then. Get up and put on your wrapper, for I shall need my sweater. And your slippers too, Sarah. But this is it—I shall put you to bed right after the picnic, and expect you to go straight to sleep!")

How could I have forgotten? *Of course!* Colin and I had gone outside for that picnic to the summerhouse. He had not thought we would need a candle, because of the full moon, but he had carried one nevertheless, "in case." And we had tiptoed downstairs together to the kitchen, where we had left the popcorn.

I rose and, slipping on my robe, slid my feet into my slippers. Tonight, unlike that other night with Colin—and there was a lamp lit in one of the bedrooms, although the door stood open, empty (*Why* couldn't I remember which one?)—there were lights under every door, but no one looked out, nor heard my soft footsteps as I descended the stairs, the graceful, curved stairs of Saramount. I carried a candle too, for I was determined to play out, so far as possible, everything that I remembered about that night.

That part of the kitchen which was in the light of the open windows did not need my candle for illumination, and my eyes were drawn to the table in the center, littered with the scattered popcorn from the open bag.

Scattered across the table, spilling out of the open bag. I looked at it, I remembered, and I knew.

CHAPTER 11

("Pick up the popcorn, Sarah, and put it back into the bag, like a good girl.")

One, two, three kernels of popcorn, dropping into the bag. One, two, three, like a series of lantern slides before my eyes, over a hiatus of twelve years, this moment, and those that followed, were relived by me. But this time I looked at them with the knowledge and the eyes of an eighteen-year-old adult.

One, two, three. Was it my breath, strangled in my throat, that threatened to suffocate me? Was it my heart, pumping blood throughout my body, that sounded in my ears like the relentless ocean pounding the beaches? Then, with a gasp, I was released from the rigid paralysis that gripped me, and in a whisper I said: "I remember. My God, I remember!"

"Yes, I thought you would, sooner or later."

He was the darkest shadow by the kitchen door. The darkest shadow in a mass of shadows, but the one that shifted, and moved, and in the light of a stray moonbeam, the one that held the gun stiffly in his hand. Now I could see his face, expressionless, with dreary, dead eyes.

"Why? Why?"

I did not know I was speaking aloud until he answered me in the same questioning voice.

"Why?" I puzzled him. I had said that I remembered, so —didn't I know why? But he could not understand that I was thinking of why it had to be Colin, gay, bright and loving; why the dreadful futility of his death?

"You mean, don't you, why I had to kill him? To prevent exposure, of course," he said simply. "It was not the first time I had killed for the same reason. Louise's death was no accident, for she came home unexpectedly one day and was upstairs before I knew it. I followed her from the house. She was hysterical and was running to find a policeman. I knew I had to stop her before she told anyone, so I pushed her under the wheels of a carriage. Luckily, her head struck the curb and she never recovered consciousness. So, you see, with Colin, I was quick to think in terms of murder. They say it is easier after the first time," he added reflectively, "but I have not found it particularly so."

We watched each other steadily, and the gun did not waver in his hand. When I made no other comment, he made a visible effort to continue.

"I guess you are puzzled about what happened. No one ever guessed how I did it. You see, he came back to his room, after he put you to bed for the second time, and I was waiting for him. I knew I had to kill him—I had come prepared with the heavy brass candlestick from my room; yet, I hoped I wouldn't have to do it. I didn't want to, you understand," he said pleadingly. "I thought he might be receptive to my persuasion, might listen to my explanations. But he turned his back on me. He was *contemptuous*. That's when I struck him. I have often wondered if he really would have talked," he added slowly. "He was only a boy, after all. But I could not take the chance."

My legs were trembling, and the little candle was quivering like a leaf between my fingers. I leaned against the table and set it down carefully, but the gun remained steady on me. But he was talking now, the words tumbling over one another, as though he felt a desperate need to purge himself by a confessional.

"I was very fond of him, you know. He was an uncommonly lovable boy. I—I—found that I was unable to remain here after his death, knowing where I buried him. I am not heartless, you see," he added querulously. "Memories—and bad dreams—all combined to haunt me. I wanted to remain away forever, but Abner insisted that I—we—return, and to refuse would have excited suspicion. I was very frightened that first day I met the young man impersonating Colin—the uncanny likeness! the talk of reviving your memory! I even had moments in which I believed —" He stopped. "All nonsense, of course. I knew he was an impostor, naturally, but I also knew that he must have a partner, and that was who I wanted. I thought of them all —all but Abner himself! I believed he was taken in, like the rest of them. Had I known—I tried desperately to find out but—and, too, I couldn't understand why he was making such an effort to bring your memory back. I concluded that he must be a blackmailer. And when I saw how close he was getting to the truth, I had to put a stop to it. It was easier to kill you, for without you, he had nothing. Nothing."

"So, instead, you killed Uncle Marion," I concluded sorrowfully.

He shrugged. The hooded eyes watched me, unblinking. "That was an error. But then, the whole thing was haphazard, subject to error. I had known I must be prepared for any contingency—the strychnine, this gun—but instead, when the subject came up again of recalling your memory, I tried, once more, with the uncertain tools that were at hand." He smiled slightly, a smile that did not reach beyond the handsome, mobile lips. "I *am* glad that I wasn't successful, Sarah. I really am very fond of you."

"As you were of Colin?" I asked bitterly.

"Exactly. And you didn't recover your memory, after all —the danger came from another source."

"Joe Bob? But why kill him? He was harmless!"

"Now, now, Sarah." For a moment, there was a glint of the old, dry humor. "You know the answer to that. You and he, together, made Joe Bob's death necessary. I was outside in the shrubbery and overheard you that night, and for the first time I realized why Joe Bob was trying to see Colin. He had been at the train station when his parents were brought home and he saw who got on the train, you see. Which little Mountain got on the train. The little red-headed Mountain children—they looked alike to so many people! The conductor never doubted that he saw Colin. He was questioned about a red-headed boy in a blue blazer, and no one thought to make sure it was the right boy."

I was not sure that I understood. "Then, Colin did not leave Saramount that night?"

"No. He was not buried until later. The early-morning hours, in fact, when I could be sure that I was not detected. And once Joe Bob heard the whole story, he knew the truth, of course. But he would not think of it being murder, since Colin had come home. That's why he had to be silenced before he talked to the false Colin."

"As *I* have to be." I eyed the gun fatalistically. All along I had been straining, hoping, to hear footsteps—Jack, anyone—to avert the certain doom that I knew was in store for me. I might fight, of course. But all along, too, I had been struggling with a dreadful lassitude that threatened to drag me under, drown me. Could I hope to fight and be successful? The gun did not waver.

"That was my intention, of course." The voice was tired, tired. "Even as late as this morning, life would have been too sweet to give up one precious moment. Although for years," he added reflectively, "I have lost everything that made it worth living. Strange . . . tonight, I find myself viewing with dread what has become, at best, an eternity of hopelessness. Tonight, in the presence of my victims, I found myself envying them . . ." His voice died away on the bitter, arid words.

I did not reply, for I was drained of speech. Although I did not understand what he meant, I knew that the decision of my death had been made: it had been considered and passed over.

He turned, his body already sagging; the outside door was pushed open with a faint whisper, and he passed through, a wraith, a shadow scarcely visible among the other shadows, the gun held stiffly in his hand.

I fled to the front hallway, where I stopped to wait, shivering and clinging to the newel post of the stairs, until I heard the shot. It was a loud, explosive report, and although I had been expecting it, I started wildly, crying out, then sank slowly to the steps as though I had received the bullet in my own body.

The sounds overhead started up immediately. The people in the bedrooms upstairs, and Grandfather in his room behind the library, had heard the noise, and the voices were agitated as they called to one another. Madeline, trailing her nightrobe behind her, found me first. She almost stumbled over me, and then bent down, her braids swinging in my face.

Jack was right behind her. "Sarah, are you hurt?" he cried hoarsely, and when I did not reply, his hands were all over me, probing, pressing.

Grandfather was next. He knelt before me. "Bring up that lamp, Victor." His worried face swam before my eyes. "What's the matter, child? Are you hurt? Was that a shot I heard?"

"It's Uncle Charles." I spoke directly to him, with an economy of words, an economy of emotion. "He used a gun. On himself. I remembered, you see."

"Is he outside?" Grandfather did not seem surprised, only relieved to find me apparently unhurt. He beckoned Victor, who was just behind Madeline, and asked him to bring up another lamp. "See to her, Jack, while we go outside."

"Don't touch me," I said mechanically. "Don't touch me."

"Let's have some light, Madeline," Jack said sharply. "I must see to her. Something is wrong."

He put his hands on me again, and this time I whirled on him savagely. "Don't touch me!" I screamed. "Don't touch me! Dirty! Dirty!"

The lamp in Madeline's hand dipped and wavered. "Keep that lamp still, you! Jack snapped. "Something is wrong here. I want to see if she's hurt!"

He reached toward me again, and this time I met him with clawing nails. "I hate you! Keep away from me!" I snarled, my lips drawn back over my teeth. Madeline gasped. "It's dirty, I tell you! It's dirty!"

Jack yanked me to my feet and pulled me strongly into his arms. Holding my hands firmly at my sides, immobilizing my ripping fingernails, he slapped me twice, hard, rocking my head backward with the force of his blows and sending me spiraling into a shower of stars. My body, which had been stiff with revulsion, crumpled, and I collapsed, limply, in his arms. He lifted me and, nodding to Madeline to precede him with the lamp, he carried me into the library, where he dumped me unceremoniously into the big leather armchair and tucked the afghan roughly around my shoulders. Kneeling before the fireplace, he touched a match to the neatly laid logs. The flames sprang up immediately, and I soon felt their grateful warmth on my face.

I was shuddering convulsively by this time. Madeline hung over me anxiously. "What's the matter with her?"

"Shock," Jack answered laconically. "She'll be all right as soon as she gets warm. And cries," he added, eying me consideringly.

"What about Uncle Charles? Is he really dead? Did he kill Colin?"

"I'm not interested in Uncle Charles," he said impatiently. "Go and see about it for yourself, if you like. I'll stay with her."

Madeline fled from the room. I did not notice her leave, for I was gazing dully into the flames, my mind as blunted as my emotions. Crouching over the fire, Jack watched me for a minute, then he gave a bitter, wordless exclamation, and slid into the chair beside me. When he pulled me into his lap I was docile, as limp and resistless as a doll.

"Sarah," he said worriedly. "Sarah, can you hear me?"

"Yes."

"Sarah, some things *are* dirty, but not the way you and I feel about each other. Only some things."

"No."

"I tell you—yes! Listen to me, Sarah, and believe what I tell you."

"No." I struggled briefly, desperately. "Where is Grandfather? I want Grandfather."

But before I could break free, the shadows came. They were elongated, wavering, on the stairwell, their bodies swaying in a ritualistic dance, as they bent over the sagging burden they carried between them. Nathan, Grandfather and Victor, with Madeline behind them, holding aloft the lamp. They passed the door, bearing the body of Uncle

Charles upstairs to his room, his head covered by a blood-stained coat.

I began shuddering again, and Jack pressed kisses lightly over my hair and forehead. Dimly, I felt comforted, but I did not want to think—about Uncle Charles, or us, or anything Uncle Charles had told me. By shutting my eyes tightly, I could shut out my thoughts. But Jack would not allow it.

"Sarah," he said insistently.

"No!"

"Yes." He whispered softly, but so close to my ear that I must hear him. "I want to tell you about what a lucky little girl you were when you were six years old." His words caught my attention so that I found myself listening, after all, trapped by their unexpectedness. "You had someone who loved you very much. He took you home and washed your face and listened to your prayers and put you to bed —just as your mother would have done. And he loved you that way—or as a brother. The right way, Sarah. You and he saw something that night—something dirty—but only he understood what it was, because you were just six years old, and he was sixteen. But he was afraid you might someday understand, so he tried very hard to make you forget. And you did forget, Sarah, my poppet, until tonight. To-night you remembered. I wonder, Sarah"—Jack's whisper stirred the hair at my ear—"could it be that he—just for tonight—came back and helped you to remember?"

I relaxed and softened, and sagged heavily against Jack, just as a baby does when he falls asleep, and grows softer and heavier in his mother's arms. His next words, when they came, did not alarm me.

"Now you are eighteen, my pet, and what you saw with Colin that night can not harm you. You must tell us now."

I looked up drowsily. The others had come in and stood

around my chair, their faces tired and worn, but no one seemed unduly shocked by what they had just witnessed. And Grandfather was smiling dimly, the tears coursing down his cheeks. I talked directly to him, like a good child making a recitation.

"He said, 'Go to sleep, Sarah, like a good girl.' And I said, 'No, please, Colin, don't leave me.' He said, 'Have your picnic tomorrow,' and I said, 'Please, Colin, don't go away. Please don't leave.' I begged so, Grandfather, and if I had not, he would still be alive."

"No, Sarah, you mustn't think of it that way," Grandfather reassured me.

"But I knew he wouldn't say no to me," I explained patiently, carefully. "I knew if I begged hard enough, he would take me to the summerhouse for a picnic. And he did. We got the popcorn and went to the summerhouse. The moon was so bright—the summerhouse was lighted by it—and we hardly needed the candle. We were very quiet and made no noise. So quiet that Uncle Charles and Rose didn't see us until we were inside. I didn't understand what they were doing. I said, 'Colin, what are they doing?' He didn't answer me. He said, 'Forget it, Sarah, and dream of tomorrow.' He talked about other things and was very pale. I thought he was sick. Then he kissed me and went to the door and said, 'Goodnight, little sister.' Then he went away."

I was exhausted. I turned my face toward Jack, burrowing into his throat, and he pulled me close. The voices went on, above my head, and I stopped listening. Gradually, the shivering stopped and the tears came, gentle, healing tears of sorrow and quiet, loving memory. Jack felt them dampening his shirt and handed me his handkerchief. A paper rustled, and I saw Jack take it from Grandfather to read, but when they spoke, carefully rationing the words they used in my presence, I didn't understand any of it.

Later, when he thought I was ready to know, Jack showed me the paper. Grandfather had found it in Uncle Charles's room that night. Apparently, Rose had left it for him to find when she was gone, and it bore evidence of having been crumpled, thrown away, and then smoothed out again, as though he had pored over it in anguish, guilt and self-hatred.

The ink was fresh, as was the paper. The lettering was rounded like a child's. I was struck anew by the dreamlike quality of it, as well as the words:

"he made me do it take colins place on the train with my hair under my cap and dressed like a boy i darent run away for he got on at the first stop and took me off there were horses waiting to take us back to saramount i didnt understand for a long time why even when colin was missing i didnt understand what we had done and when i did i became everything he had made of me

"because of colin you see i thought i hated colin because he was so good but after he died i knew i just wanted someone like colin to love me rose is wicked and sly but i love colin i love colin because he is so good"

He encourages me to talk about it. I think he worries that if I am silent, I will brood. To him, our days at Saramount were a boon, a gift, a precious period of time that nothing can replace. For his sake, I am happy that it is so. But sometimes, especially in the spring, my mind drifts back. I look at him and see stamped on his face the unformed, rounded features of a boy: the hair, the eyes the same, the smile softer, sweeter, and then—I remember Colin.

Lillian Cheatham lives with her husband
in Columbia, South Carolina.
She is the author of two Crime Club novels,
The Marriage Pact and *Portrait of Emma*.